Blue Fire

Angela Castle

Dedication

To my friends who patiently listened to my plots
and allowed me to badger them for ideas and solutions.

Prologue

Crystal City
Land of the Kell

Claws dug into Drystan's arm. He swung his blade round his head, twisting his large body. Drystan, the commander of the Kell army, kicked high into the lizard-like man's underbelly then shoved the body away. The Drac Scoull left bloody scratch marks as it was hurtled onto its back. Drystan did not hesitate, his blade sunk all the way into the exposed side of the Scoull's armour. The enemy gave a high pitched squeal, its body convulsing in its death throes. He yanked the blade out and ran forward to the next target; blood and adrenaline coursed through his system. His heart, full of anguish and rage, pounded so hard against his ribs he feared it would explode. So many Drac Scoulls in the way.

The screams of the women echoed around him. *Oh, by the gods.* He fought not for his life but for theirs. The city had been left unguarded; the Drac Scoulls had stormed the inner city. In and out of every home they had gone. Drystan had witnessed them dragging out the women, the helpless babes, the young girls, to slaughter them. The streets were running red with their blood.

The army had been too far away, lured out to battle by Norlac, ruler of the Drac. Adalardo, King of the Kells, had seized the opportunity to end the war once and for all. Every able-bodied man had marched on the Drac fortress.

The Drac were like a swarm of insects moving in every direction. Drystan leapt over the body of an adolescent girl. His blade again hitting its mark; another Scoull's head went flying. His hard, muscled body ached from exertion and was dripping with sweat; his body armour was splattered with blood. He battled, until there were none left to kill.

"That has to be the entire Drac army," panted Melor, who had been fighting a step behind him.

"Go, keep searching. Do not rest until we know every Scoull is dead. May the gods have spared some of our women from this horror."

Melor nodded, racing off. Adalardo came hurtling around the corner on the back of his stag; his own face dark with the same anguished rage Drystan was feeling.

"Drystan, to the palace! There are still Scoulls inside." He bolted towards the Palace gate tower. Drystan raced behind his King. He hoped and prayed there were some still alive.

Long after the fall of darkness, the air hung in heavy silence. They had come too late. A handful of older women had been found in the deeper dungeon of the Palace. They had locked themselves in to escape the Drac. Glow crystals were lit to assist with what needed to be done. There would be no rest tonight. A heavy toll had befallen the people of Kell. It had cost them their women; all of the female population, along with some younger male children, slaughtered. Even the King himself assisted with the moving of bodies, the pain in his face evident as he passed Drystan. The burden of his crown weighed heavier at this time than any other. With the palace cleared, the king called on his men once more.

"There can be no more great numbers of Scoulls than what we killed here this eve." He drew in a breath, his rage barely contained. "They have used the last of their greater numbers to inflict this wound upon us, but I for one will not sit and mourn until every last Drac's blood flows from its disembowel body." There were nods of approval, grunts of eagerness, the men wanted revenge on the Drac. Drystan wanted to peel the flesh from Norlac's body, to hear him scream, just like he had made their women scream as his Drac Scoull's had murdered them.

"They will not be expecting another attack so soon." Drystan rose to his feet, glancing at the King. "The men will be ready within the hour. This time we will not leave one stone in place on Norlac's Fortress." He turned to survey the crowed of strong, hardened Warriors, every one trained under his supervision. The expectation of sweet revenge was written on their features. "To battle!" Drystan cried, thrusting his sword into the air. They hurried, making preparations for the coming final battle.

"I pray my friend; this will be the end of the war." The King walked to stand by his side. "We now have a new battle to wage." Drystan knew exactly what he meant. Their very survival as a race was now in jeopardy. Without women, the Kell's were doomed to die out. Their people teetered on the brink of extinction.

Chapter One

Lloyd Mountain
Tasmania, Australia

Jane gripped the steering wheel with her right hand, the now crumpled map in her left. Her gaze darted from the map to the road as her 'Walkers' Cleaning Service van crawled along the dirt track. It had taken her two hours to get from the outer suburbs of Hobart. The time was ticking away. She didn't want to keep her client waiting.

"*Mt. Lloyd is a fair drive. Are you sure there isn't anyone closer, Mr. Richards? I usually only service the inner suburbs of Hobart.*"

The man had snapped a quick, "*No. I'll reimburse any travelling costs.*" It tipped it for Jane as she scribbled it into her diary. She didn't have another job till Thursday, and today was Tuesday.

The van hit a ditch, pitching her forward onto the steering wheel with a humph. The map was tossed aside as she clutched the van's wheel with both hands to keep it steady on the road. Spotting a gate up ahead, she sighed with relief. There were two signs: one was strung up on the gate itself, another sign placed atop a metal post which read:

"State Forest. Trespassers Prosecuted."

On the older, wooden sign wired to the gate carved in big bold letters she read **"Tindayle Cottage**, *'point of no return'*." Some smart alec had spray painted the last few words in red. Jane rolled her eyes. Tasmania was known for its ghosts, but Jane was a firm believer in 'if you could see and touch it, then it existed'. The rest was all nonsense.

Jane smiled in relief. At least her lousy sense of direction hadn't gotten her lost this time. Jane always allowed herself plenty of what she called 'lost' time before a new job in order to find it properly.

As she neared the fence, Jane noticed that this road had not been used in a while. The tall, native trees of the forest filtered beams of sunlight, giving an almost ethereal gleam to the beautiful surroundings-- the shadows, trees, rocks and shrubs of the native Tasmanian Forest.

Jane pulled on the parking brake, shoved the gear into neutral, and climbed out of the van to open the gate. It required a forceful shove to make it move. If the unused track was any indicator of time, the cottage would be in a right state.

"Think about the money, think about the money," she muttered aloud, heading back to the van to drive it through the gate. Jane did the right thing by closing the gate behind her. She didn't want to get into trouble with the local farmers over gates left open, allowing domestic animals to wander into the forest due to her recklessness.

It was a long, slow, bumpy ride up into the mountain's thick forest before Jane made a hard left turn into a clearing. Finally the house came into view, looming up out of the trees.

Jane pulled up and sat gazing at the old, double-storey, colonial building. There was one central door with mirroring windows on either side, almost the same length as the door itself. The upper balcony had the same structure. Despite its obvious age, it still looked solid. Jane had stopped directly in front of the broken-down, brown picket fence. She hoped they didn't expect her to mend that.

Climbing out to wander, she walked to the first window to peer in. Even in the dim haze she could see a right mess in the first room. Oh yes, it was going to be a heck of a job. If Mr. Richards wanted this cottage sparkling, he would have to pay.

The sound of an engine followed by the blaring of a car horn broke the tranquillity of the surroundings. Up the drive came a shiny gold Mercedes. Gravel flew as the car skidded to a halt behind Jane's van. A tall, well-dressed businessman with fair hair and deep blue eyes emerged. He flashed the fakest smile she had ever seen--a cheesy *'I'll sell Ice to Eskimos'* real estate agent smile. As he glanced her over, Jane instantly knew the expression that flashed across his face. It was a 'you're-an-ugly-fat-chick' look. Something Jane was used to. He had spotted the name embroidered on her navy blue t-shirt. She struggled not to glower at the man, keeping a pleasant smile on her face.

"Jane. So glad you found your way without any trouble. So what do you think?" He had turned back to stare at the old building.

"Beautiful old place."

"Oh, yeah a beauty. Got high hopes for this one. Houses with great stories sure sell pretty well."

Jane got the feeling he was talking more to himself than to her. "What's this one's story?"

"Mysterious vanishings, hauntings, the usual thing in Tasmania." The brief explanation did little to satisfy her curiosity.

"It's easy to get lost in a forest," Jane said. Mr. Richards shrugged. A good salesman would hype up any story if it would help to sell the house better. But Jane was not a potential buyer, so he didn't bother.

"So, how much for the cleaning?" He pressed her back into business mode.

"I'll need to have a look through then I can give you a price."

He unhooked an old brass key from a chain of keys he'd pulled from his pocket before leading the way to the front door. He shoved the heavy door open with his shoulder before stepping back to let Jane in.

"I'll wait here," he muttered and wrinkled his nose before proceeding to dust himself down. Jane wandered through to examine the interior. Internally, the building was in rather good shape, just neglected, with dust everywhere and a few scatterings of old furniture. There were also some stains on the lower walls which resembled the colour of dark tea. It had three upper bedrooms with polished wooden floors, a converted bathroom to the rear which needed a good muck out, and the kitchen that needed every inch scrubbed.

"Two days," Jane finally told the man as she re-emerged at the front door, "It will take me twenty-four hours and with travel costs--it will be seven hundred and fifty." She avoided eye contact. Jane had always hated discussing money. But it was a necessary part of the job. If he didn't like it…Jane hoped he would be okay with it. She had already spent eighty dollars on fuel. She wanted the work.

"Fine," he said without blinking. He was looking at her now like, well, the hired help she was. He withdrew his wallet. Jane had to keep her bottom jaw from dropping as he withdrew a wad of cash from an

7

overstuffed wallet. He counted out her fee then handed over the green and gold notes.

"You don't have to…"

"I'll pay you now." He cut her off. "I won't be back to the property for a few days. You can drop the key off at my office." He also handed her his agency card along with a large brass key.

"I'll get you a receipt." She was backing towards the van to grab her little invoice book.

"Drop the receipt off at the agency too," he said in an I-don't-want-to-stick-around-here-any–longer-dealing-with-domestic-staff tone.

Jane forced herself to smile at him. "The place will sparkle when I'm finished here." The man didn't acknowledge the comment. He was already striding to his car. A moment later his expensive, imported car was gone from view. Jane let out a sigh of relief as she was left to the peaceful sounds of the forest. Jane spun round on her heel, sizing up the big, old house once again.

"Right. Let's get this done!"

~ * ~

Adalardo, King of Kell, sat in his throne room. The raised platform of his chair gave him height above the crowd of men standing before him. They were sectioned off in groups, according to their classes. Drystan leaned against the wall and watched the heated arguments between the classes. The noise echoed off the high ceiling. He felt more useless than he ever had in his long war career. Swords he understood. Fighting he understood. Finding women to secure a future for his people? He was at a loss.

"My King, what is to be done?" Arland, the head council of the scholar classes spoke first.

Adalardo drew himself to his feet. The other groups turned to look at him.

"How many women remain in the kingdom?" Adalardo turned his gaze in Drystan's direction. He, with his warriors, had spent the past season searching every inch of the Kell kingdom.

Drystan stood up straight to speak to the assembly. "There are thirteen females in the kingdom, your majesty. Two infants, and the others are all too old to bear children," Drystan reported.

Adalardo nodded grimly. This did not bode well for their people. "Raise the infants with care. There will be no promising any of the young ones until they are of age." There was a slight grumble--securing a mate was vital for survival. This decree would stop men fighting each other to obtain a wife-promise for a while.

Drystan watched the assembly that had come to consult with the King regarding the lack of women. The war had taken a terrible toll on all of the Kell people. The land and people needed healing.

Two seasons had now passed. Slowly they had begun to rebuild, sow the land, and move forward, but the evident loneliness was growing. Something needed to be done, and the men needed wives. The land needed children.

The class groups looked at their King in hope. Drystan understood Adalardo was determined to secure the future of his people as much as he was. The only question was how?

"Patience, my good subjects," he told those gathered. "I have decided to consult with our Sorcerer. There may be something his magic can do. I will call another gathering when there is more to discuss." The meeting ended. The groups gave their King a respectful bow before moving towards the exit of the throne chamber, murmuring among themselves. The only man left was Drystan. As the King had no heir, the throne would fall to Drystan if anything should befall Adalardo. It was not a task Drystan wanted. He led the army not the land.

"What makes you think Tuathal can help?" Drystan ran his hand through his black hair to smooth back a lock that had fallen forward.

"Do you have a better suggestion?" Adalardo stepped down from the throne dais. "Maybe he knows a place we have failed to search. At this time I am willing to try any magic, give anything to ensure we have a future."

"I am not convinced magic can bring us women." Drystan was sceptical of Sorcerer magic. Though its presence was acknowledged, it was considered an act of cowardice to use magic in battle. The Sorcerer class were few. They kept to themselves, never offering aid to anyone, but always, for the right price, willing to assist any Kell who came to them for help. Adalardo put his hand on his friend's shoulder.

"You will come?" Drystan nodded, for he knew anything was worth a try.

~ * ~

Tuathal, Sorcerer of Kell, dwelt in a tall tower, east, along the coast. The tower stood at the mouth of the San-Rah River on a small island. A causeway of large stepping stones connected the main land to the island. They left their stags by the riverbank and followed the path down towards the tower. Both of Kell's Moons had risen, giving clear sight for every footstep. Drystan looked back to his stag, feeling vulnerable, almost naked without his sword. The one thing Drystan knew he could always rely on was cold, hard steel. The King too had left his behind. They both knew Tuathal would not tolerate weapons within his presence. As they approached the base of the tower, the door opened automatically. Tuathal was obviously welcoming them. Glow crystals above the door showed the way. Once inside the door, they started up the spiral staircase. They came to the first platform. A large, round table dominated the room, and a thick heavy violet curtain covered one quarter of the room, hanging from the base of the next stairs winding up to another level toward one of the two windows. Four chairs were around the table, and a pile of crystals and scrolls were strewn across the table top. Fire crystals heated the room from a hearth facing the near wall of the stairs, taking the chill from the cold night air.

Tuathal drew back the curtain, and stepped into the room. Despite the Sorcerer's old age, Tuathal had a youthful look. He had chiseled handsome features. A scar ran downward under his left eye, which was not black like his right but was an eerie glowing amber.

Rumour had it he had sold his soul to the dark forces to obtain his magical powers then had battled the devil himself to steal it back.

"I know why you're here." Tuathal's rich voice was the first to break the silence.

"Can you help us, help the people of Kell?" Adalardo got straight to the point.

"I will not raise the dead, for it has too many evil complications. What you need is fresh blood, women of a new generation from a different land."

Drystan frowned. Sorcerers were also known for their cryptic natures. "We have searched all the land, there are..."

"Some worlds are beyond what you can see," Tuathal cut him off.

Adalardo drew in a breath, trying to ebb his frustration. "Do these other worlds have what we need?"

Tuathal nodded, a smile twitched at the corner of his mouth. "Women of rare beauty," the smile faded, "accessing these worlds is extremely difficult. Only those who have travelled through a portal can move back and forth."

"And you have?" Drystan did not bother to hide the scepticism in his voice.

Tuathal choose to ignore Drystan's cynical question. "Others have come through portals, with visions in their heads of bountiful lands . It was unfortunate they did not survive. The journey though these portals is fraught with great peril. The ones I found were gravely injured and died before any healing could be administered." The Sorcerer turned to pick up a long staff with a glowing crystal that had been resting against the wall; the crystal matched the amber of his left eye. "If you find me one alive, I will create a doorway between our worlds."

"How are we to find them? Where do we look?" Adalardo stepped closer to the Sorcerer.

"The ones I have found were near the Blue Forest and the Crystal Violet Mountains, but they could be anywhere."

Drystan glared at the sorcerer. They were to look for someone who may not exist, who may come through a portal that may not exist. "This does us no good. It is an impossible thing. If what you say is true, then such a person my never appear." Drystan was frustrated; coming to see Tuathal was a waste of time.

Tuathal's mismatched eyes turned on him. "For now it is all I have to offer. May I add, for free? But the next part will come at a price."

"If there is a next part."

Tuathal gave him a half-knowing smile. What was he not saying? Drystan fought the urge to grab the sorcerer and beat him into giving a straight answer.

"Oh there will be," Tuathal said seemingly self-assured there was more to

come.

Chapter Two

Jane's arm ached. She had worked hard through the day, scrubbing, cleaning, carting water up the stone steps from three hundred meters below. Mr. Richards had forgotten to mention there was no running water. The old, rusty tank at the back had a huge hole in it, leaving Jane to search for a new source of water. Following the sound of rushing water, she had found a pleasant creek and a few feet away she discovered a little waterfall, gushing from a crack in two huge boulders. The Australian forest was beautiful, but she hated the fact she had to trudge up and down the steps with the water buckets, adding to the day's torture of physical labor.

Now it was getting dark. She had stayed longer than intended. Home was a two hour drive. Jane's whole body was sagging with fatigue. Maybe driving for two hours was not a good idea.

"Drowsy Drivers Die" announced the signs posted all along the freeway. Staying the night in the empty old house was the most logical idea.

"No one will know." She was talking aloud to herself again, a habit she had developed due to spending a lot of time by herself. "I can have the rest finished early in the morning then take the rest of the day off." Jane smiled to herself. Ripping off her pink rubber gloves, she headed out to the van.

A good boy scout is always prepared. Not that she had ever been one. In the side wing of her van were a few blankets, air mattress, kettle, and small supply of cookies, chocolate bars, and coffee-the instant kind with milk powder already mixed in. 'Just add hot water,' the pack said. Jane loved them. She carried them into the front living room of the cottage, onto the newly clean floors. After rolling out the air mattress, she set everything else up by the fire place.

Right, she would need wood and water. She prayed the chimney was clear enough to light a fire. She knew how cold it could get up in the Tasmanian Mountains.

After gathering enough wood to last the night, Jane pushed her wayward plain brown hair out of her eyes, grabbed her flashlight and bucket then walked out the back door of the cottage. One more trip to the creek to fetch water. The light had almost faded as she ascended the stone steps carefully. It was easier to fall over in the dark and no one knew she was up here, apart from Mr. Richards. She was sure if she fell and broke something help would not come readily. Dark shadows formed everywhere. Jane shivered, a little frightened, hoping the haunting stories were limited to the house. Her wild imagination always seemed to come to life at night, with the thought of wild mountain creatures.

She laughed out loud. "Wild mountain creatures?" This was Tasmania for goodness sake. Possums, kangaroos, maybe the occasional

Tasmanian devil--there were no wild beasts which could kill or maim. It was too cold for snakes, and she'd cleaned the cottage well enough to be free of spiders and other insects.

A rustle of leaves startled her. Her heart thudded in her chest with a sudden fear of the unknown. She swung around, aiming her flashlight at the sound. The glint of a wallaby's eyes flashed back. Jane let out a breath she didn't know she was holding.

"Hello," she told the marsupial in a soft, gentle voice, after her heart had come down from the sudden high. It looked at her then limped away. Limped? Oh, the poor little thing was injured. Jane stupidly started cooing at the marsupial. "You're hurt, come here little one. I can help you." The wallaby stopped again and limped a little further up the side of the mountain. Jane followed. She wanted to help the creature . See where it was injured, maybe clean the wound and bandage it. She had always wanted to be a vet. As a child she had all manner of creatures for pets. But in one way or the other, by the time she had morphed into a confused teenager, they had all died. Not to mention she didn't have enough self confidence to have a go at college. All Jane knew how to do was clean and she had made a reasonable living out-sourcing her services to others.

Jane went after the wallaby, moving slowly so she didn't scare it. Maybe she should get some food to entice it. She stepped around a large boulder, keeping her flashlight pointing at the ground so as not to trip. She had just walked into the entrance of a small cave. Water from the creek trickled into it from outside, making a small flow near the entrance along the rock. The shine from the torch hit the water, reflecting the light. She heard movement up ahead .Jane raised her flashlight at the wallaby.

"It's alright." She cooed, taking a step onto wet rock. "It'll be..." Jane's foot hit slick slime from the wet rock. She slid forward, losing her balance and falling backward. The moment her bottom hit the wet rock, a scream tore from her throat as her body was propelled downward, sliding helplessly into the cave. The torch flew from her hand as she desperately tried to grab on to anything. It was all slippery and wet. Freezing cold water drenched her from head to toe. As she fell, Jane screamed again, terrified, in this never-ending plunge downward. Jane's head hit a rock with a thick thud. She reeled, grunting in pain. Her eyes were heavy as her entire body went limp, blacking out.

~ * ~

CLANG, SWOOSH, CLANG!

Drystan's sword met his opponent's thrust, parrying before lunging, throwing his weight behind the sword and pushing the warrior in training off balance. Gravel sprayed over Drystan's freshly polished boot as the man hit the ground with a thud.

"Always keep your feet planted," he said, instructing those who watched from the sidelines. War or no war, he would keep up the training for his men. He wanted to keep their skills honed and ready.

"Commander!" Melor, one of Drystan's elite, ran into the training yard.

Drystan had been working out his fury with his sword and his warriors. His mind had been pondering what course of action to take since returning from the sorcerer tower.

"Several Drac Scoulls have been seen to the west of the Blue Forest."

Drystan's blood heated at the news, his hands itching for a fight. Drystan had been enraged that Norlac had escaped the Kell retribution when they had taken and destroyed the Drac fortress. He wanted vengeance on their leader.

"Crystal gatherers saw them while passing on the western trail." Melor finished his report.

"Gather a patrol. We head out in half an hour," Drystan snapped. Melor had already turned on his heels, barking orders to the servants who waited nearby. Drystan headed into the palace to inform the King--he would want in on this action.

It wasn't long before seven men galloped out behind Adalardo and Drystan, heading westward toward the Blue Forest. Riding their stags hard for an hour, the men passed through the twin moon valley. A river gracefully twisted its way through the valley giving life to lush green fields. They came into a lightly wooded area of blue Fherr-loin trees at the base of the Blue Forest ranges.

The trail of the crystal gatherers moved from the city up into the mountains. Crystals were the life-blood of the Kells, a vital source of energy, light, heating, healing and magic, interwoven into the fabric of their buildings and homes. This area was a remote, uninhabited part of the gatherer's expeditions.

The higher they climbed into the mountainous area, the thicker the trees became. Large boulders protruded from the ground. It was a good area in which to mount an ambush on an enemy, Drystan noted.

18

Drystan pulled his stag to a stop and dismounted. The men followed suit.

"It will be easier to search on foot, lest they hear the sound of the stag's hooves." His men spread out. Silent and deadly, his warriors began moving in search of their hated enemy.

~ * ~

Jane's head hurt terribly. A dull thumping pounded through her temple. Oh god, she must be dead. Her eyes opened slightly, bright light streamed in, and her brain screamed for her to shut her eyes again. She obeyed. She was aware other parts of her body were in pain as she tried to move her limbs. The lower part of Jane's body was submerged in water . It lapped gently around her waist. Her head was pressed against the dirt. Not sure where she was, Jane forced open her eyes. Despite the pain, she looked around. She was in a cave, the ceiling reaching a few meters above and about five meters wide. Her right leg throbbed . It must have been bruised during the fall. Oh god, she had fallen. Last night. She must have been unconscious all night in this underground pool.

Drawing herself to her knees, Jane slowly crawled towards the light of the cave's entrance. Cripes, she must have a concussion, her head throbbed more as she finally came out of the mouth of the cave. "Have to get back to the van," she told herself. She'd use her cell phone to call for help. Jane glanced briefly around. Nothing looked familiar. How far had she fallen, she wondered. Should she go up or down the hill? She couldn't think.

19

She slid her legs around until they came out in front of her. The pain in her right side was bad. She whimpered and lifted up her shirt slightly to see if she was bleeding. A huge purplish, yellow bruise marred her whole right side. Jane was no medic but had seen enough hospital TV shows to know she was injured internally. She needed to get to a hospital. She wasn't sure how much more of this pain she could take. But she had to. Jane needed to keep going, didn't she? Her life depended on it.

"Friggen wallabies!" she muttered. Never again would she try to help a hurt animal. Cursing the wallaby gave her a bit of strength. Bracing herself, she stood up. Pain shot down her side. Whimpering, she grabbed onto the rock beside her. Jane made a decision. Down. She was going down. There had to be houses somewhere at the base of the mountain. She had seen them driving up. Any climbing would probably make her injuries worse.

Jane waited for the pain to subside before taking several steps forward . She reached out to grip onto a nearby tree then spied the next tree she could hang on to. A white one with blue leaves. Taking another two steps, Jane reached out for it. "Aauugh!" The pain brought tears to her eyes. She panted and waited for the pain to ease.

White tree, blue leaves? What? She looked up at the odd tree she now clung to. At no time in her life had Jane ever seen a tree like this. The bark was soft beneath her fingers, the bristle-like leaves a silvery-blue. Wow. Had she discovered a new species of plant while lost in the great Tasmanian wilderness? The headlines flashed in her mind.

"Fat cleaning lady finds new exotic Tasmanian plant before dying of exposure."

"Friggen, brilliant!" Jane muttered aloud. "Come on, girl." Talking aloud gave her some more strength to keep going. "Live to get on the front cover of National Geographic." Jane launched herself forward once again.

The game of grab and hold onto a tree, rest then keep going, tired Jane's body quickly. She was not as fit as she would like to have been. Her cleaning business had done wonders to help her lose weight, as cleaning involved lots of physical labor. Jane called her jobs exercise routines. She had lost ten pounds from her former self. It was a great motivator to keep on going at it. Jane had dropped two dress sizes, going from a size eighteen to a fourteen. But she still felt fat, unattractive. She had given up hope of ever being skinny the day she first tasted chocolate. She was too addicted to chocolate biscuits, yummy candies, coconut balls, and chocolate crackles. Gaawwd, at twenty-eight would she never grow up?

Jane braced herself again. Trying hard to ignore the pain ripping through her side and the throbbing in her head, she pressed on.

The thought of the food had made Jane's stomach rumble. Oh great! Now she was hungry? Her mouth was dry and her throat parched. What time was it anyway? She looked down at her wrist watch. It wasn't there. The darn thing must have snapped off in the fall.

A noise caught Jane's attention. She froze, stilling her breathing in order to hear better. She listened. Nothing. Hairs pricked up on the back of Jane's neck. Someone or something was out there.

"Hello? Oh god, is there anyone there?" Her gaze darted round, and she hoped for signs of something, anything. Jane couldn't take it any longer. She cried out in despair.

"Help!" Her voice croaked. "Please, someone help me!" She yelled louder on the last word. Then stopped, listened.... nothing but the sound of her heart pounding in her chest. Footsteps. Someone *was* there! Relief flooded though her as she sagged against the tree. She called out again. Another moment ticked by.

A wave of dizziness hit Jane. She groaned, dropping her head down. She heard footsteps on the leaf-covered ground. She couldn't raise her head. Trying madly to combat another wave of dizziness, Jane lost her grip on the tree. She fell. She was falling. But the impact of the ground never came. Someone had caught her, hadn't they?

Jane felt safe. Yes, she had been rescued. Someone was talking--a deep, rich, husky baritone. She opened her eyes slowly, wanting to see the owner of such a vibrantly masculine voice. She looked up at her dark and devastatingly handsome rescuer. Piercing dark eyes . Black eyes like the depths of the night. They were unlike anything she'd ever seen before. I'm delirious, she thought. But what a nice delirium to be in. Jane could fight it no longer . Exhaustion and pain were taking their toll on her battered body. She again slipped into a dark unconsciousness.

Chapter Three

Never in all his seasons had he seen someone with quite so much color on them as the woman he held in his arms. Drystan heard the voice yelling--a feminine voice, pained and desperate. All his men had heard it as they started their climb from the base of the Blue Mountain. Quickly, silently, they moved in on the sound as to not alert any nearby enemy if this was a trap. Then he spotted her, gripping on to a Ferr-loin tree, her shoulder-length light brown hair dancing with red-fire highlights which shone in the sun. Her skin was pale and creamy. Although she wore the turrets of a male below her waist, she had the unmistakable curved outline of a female. The gentle curves of her breasts under her tight garment were plain to see. A woman. She was injured.

Without another thought, Drystan darted forward, catching the woman before she hit the ground. Her warmth flooded though him on contact. Feeling the woman's body in his arms was almost a shock to his system. Dry blood stuck her beautiful hair to the left side of her temple. Perspiration beaded on her pale forehead. She had high feminine cheekbones and a lovely oval face. Her long eyelashes cast a faint shadow on her cheek. She opened her eyes. Her lush pink lips parted. She uttered something in a language he did not understand. Her pale blue eyes were glazed over in pain as she gazed briefly up at him before they closed again. He was rocked by their color. Gods, they were beauty incarnate.

"I've never seen such light colored hair," Adalardo said, reaching out, gently sliding it between his finger tips. He was as mesmerized by the girl as all the warriors were. Drystan and Adalardo shared a knowing look. Could this be the kind of person Tuathal had spoken of?

Drystan tore his gaze away from the beauty to look at the men. Oh yes. They looked at her like she was the promise of water after three long days in the *Sun-Rah* desert.

"She's so, so…. small." It was Melor who spoke. "Where do you think she came from?"

"Scout the area. See if there is anyone else. She may have an attacker." Adalardo's orders brought their attention back to why they were out here. "Drystan, take care of the girl." The King, along with Drystan's elite warriors, melted back into the forest.

Drystan lifted the girl with ease, marveling at how light she was. Kell women were almost as tall as the men but more heavily set. The rounder, plumper the female the more she was prized, in order to keep their men warm at night. Drystan carried this girl easily back down to where they had left the stags.

Setting her down by a tree, he quickly lay down his fur cloak and fetched the healing crystals and a water pouch from his saddle bag. He gently lifted the girl, laying her down on the furs. Cradling her head with one hand, he poured a drop into her mouth. She coughed, spluttered, and mumbled something before her head lolled back again. Drystan wanted to touch her. He gently swept the dishevelled hair away from her forehead, the strands silky to his touch. Then he ran a finger down her jaw line. The pale skin was so smooth and soft. Drystan wanted to touch and feel the rest of her to see if she was as smooth and soft all over.

An unexpected outburst of possessiveness surprised and worried him. Drystan had never been possessive of anything but his sword. Before the Drac attack, willing women had come and gone from his bed, but war and the protection of his people had been his life. He gave a low growl. Whoever had hurt her would pay dearly. He removed the six healing crystals from his small leather pouch. Placing one on the woman's forehead, and one on of each in her palms, he lifted the material up from her waist, revealing soft, tight, creamy skin marred with a horrid purplish-yellow bruise. He placed the crystal at the waist band of her turrets and one on each of her lower legs. When the crystals aligned, they connected, creating a high pitched humming sound which started the process. An illuminated mist appeared, swirling its way around the beautifully voluptuous woman, snaking its way up until it covered her whole body. A moan escaped the girl's lips. The stones were healing her inner and outer body. When she opened her eyes for a second time, a breath caught in Drystan's throat. Desire shot through him like a wild fire making his turrets feel tight.

"Sleep," he whispered huskily. Her delicate eyelashes fluttered closed. He missed her eyes. He felt himself wanting to awaken her again so he could see them. Drystan gently lifted the crystals from their places and covered her with the furs before forcing himself to move back.

To distract himself from the sleeping girl, he busied himself with making a small fire to warm against the chill and cooking a few pieces of meat one of the servants had hurriedly packed in their haste to get out. He would have to be on his guard in case there were any Drac Scoulls about. Protecting the girl was his highest priority. He sat down finally. It was a simple pleasure to watch her sleep.

~ * ~

Jane purred in a contented sleepy haze then rolled from her back onto her side. What a nightmare--the falling, the pain. Jane gave a shudder at the memory of it. Yet she remembered her rescuer's handsome face and eyes black as midnight. She lay on something soft and luxurious. It felt like fur, a thick warm fur that held a heady spicy male scent. Dreamily, her eyes opened slightly, her gaze falling on her large, muscled rescuer. The man of her dreams. Oh, she was definitely still dreaming. He had square, god-like features, the kind which belonged on the cover of GQ rather than in her dreams. Deep-set black eyes, with luxurious thick, black hair fell about his ears--perfect for gliding her fingers through.

His glorious lips curled into a smile as he looked at her with…desire? Mmmm…it was her dream so yes, desire. He wanted her. She wanted him.

Jane gave a seductive smile back. Arching her back, stretching her arms above her head like a cat, she beckoned her tall, dark, handsome dream man forward to her. Jane hoped she wouldn't wake up before she could feel him kiss her.

He seemed to hesitate for a moment. He rocked forward to his knees, lowering himself down. Closer, closer. The scent of his raw, aroused masculinity flooded her senses, making Jane's whole body tingle with promise. Her every nerve ending was alive, waiting, wanting to be touched. She felt her nipples harden into points. Moisture pooled between her legs, an aching need developing like never before, a need she didn't understand. But she didn't need to in her dream.

She parted her lips, her tongue darting out to moisten them. His strong arm came to rest to the left of her head, supporting his weight, as he now hovered just above her. She reached her fingers up, running them along the thick, hard muscle of his right shoulder, delighting Jane no end. His arm bent, bringing him closer to her still, his warm breath sending shivers of delight down her spine. He was staring at her lips.

Kiss me, kiss me, kiss me! she willed. As if in answer, he swooped the final distance, claiming her lips. White-hot searing pleasure shot though Jane on contact. Down into her mouth he went. Over and over again he pushed his tongue past Jane's teeth, stroked inside, took, and demanded. Pure desire fogged her senses. He tasted of exotic spices. She uttered a low needy moan. The flavor of him was intoxicating, addictive. Never in all the dull reality of her life had Jane been kissed like this. Jane wanted this dream kiss to last forever. She wanted this dream man.

Somewhere in the haze, a twig snapped. Her dream man tore from her, jumping up in one fluid movement. Drawing a god for honest *'I'll slice-you-in-two'* sword.

Jane snapped suddenly out of her dreamy, lust haze, realizing she had not been dreaming at all. Gasping in shock, her heart pounded in her chest as she scrambled to her feet. Reality hit her harder than a semi truck. She had been kissing this tall, muscle-bound, sword-wielding hulk. She barely reached his shoulder. He uttered something in a low voice she didn't understand. He reached out, shoving her behind him, not that Jane could see whatever it was he wanted to protect her from. Shuffling backward, tripping on the furs, she fell with a thump on her backside, between the hulk's tree trunk legs. She could see exactly the cause of the problem. Two greenish-blue lizard-like men were stalking forward. The first one had its yellowish reptilian eyes fixed on the warrior man in front of her. The other had a murderous gaze locked on her!

Jane swallowed. It was very clear these creatures were not friendly. Fear and adrenalin shot through Jane's system. Her *'fight or flight'* instincts were telling her to run, but she couldn't seem to move her feet. With two large lizard creatures against one hulk, it was evident the odds were in the lizard men's favor. No. She wasn't going to run. She'd be damned if she was going to die a helpless victim of weird creatures who looked like they came out of the imagination of a horror film maker.

This was no movie though. This was real, deadly. The gleam of a jewelled dagger strapped to the hulk's waist band caught her eye. A weapon. Scrambling to her feet, she grabbed it from his belt.

The hulk gave a low growl, never taking his eyes from the approaching creatures. He uttered something she didn't understand, again shoving her behind him. No sooner had he done this than the two creatures charged forward. The second moving to the left as the first one leapt, his deadly blade raised to strike. Her hulk was already deflecting.

CLANG! The sound reverberated, sending a shock wave through Jane's system. She tightly gripped the hilt of the dagger.

Jane scrambled to the right. She backed up against the trunk of a large blue tree, watching the fight with horror. The first creature swung his blade with a *whoosh* towards the large man. Jane's hunk danced out of the way, but the second creature charged in low from the left, knocking the hulk off balance. He scarcely avoided another swipe of the sword from the first creature. As he fell to the ground, he rolled to avoid being impaled by another thrust of the lizard creature's blade. His sword shot out, slashing the lower leg of the second creature. It fell back, screeching in pain.

Jane winced at the horrid sound and covered her ears. The first lizard man jumped on top of the hulk, trying to bring its blade down into

28

the hulk's neck. It was then Jane spotted her opportunity. She leapt forward, raised the dagger and brought it down with all the force she could muster. The blade sank into the partly-clothed scaly back. The creature howled and arched back, its arms twisted around, trying desperately to grab at the dagger she had embedded in him. Jane stumbled back as her hulk threw the creature off.

Jane was suddenly hit from the side and flung to the ground. The impact knocked the breath from her lungs. She was momentarily dazed and tried to regain her senses with a shake of her head. Jane glanced up just in time to see the flash of the lizard man's sword descending upon her. She quickly curled her leg and kicked at his ankle with all her strength. It must have been a soft spot, as it screeched before toppling forward. Jane rolled away before the creature fell on her. Its blade went hurtling to her right side. Without hesitation or thought, she snatched up the sword, scrambled to her knees, and thrust the blade straight into the creature's chest then yanked it out. The creature thrashed about for a moment before it stilled completely. Breathing hard, her whole body was shaking as she stumbled to her feet.

What in hell had happened to mild-mannered, timid little Jane? What was wrong with her? First kissing a complete stranger and now killing a lizard creature. Her whole world had fallen into some kind of horrible nightmare. Jane suddenly felt light-headed. Letting go of the sword still in her hand, she watched it drop to the ground with a clatter.

"*Perr-ta.*" Fingers brushed Jane's arm. She turned to glance up into the hulk's smiling dark eyes. He seemed to be looking at her with admiration and pride. This expression was something she had never before experienced from anyone, not even her parents. So many emotions hit Jane at once, she was unable to stop the tears from spilling down her cheeks. "*Perr-ta.*" He cooed gently, wiping her tears with the pad of his calloused thumb before pulling her into his embrace.

Here Jane felt safe and comforted, enjoying his divine masculine scent . She let her eyes flutter closed and relaxed into his warm strong arms. The hulk scooped her up and carried her as if she weighed less than a bag of feathers. Jane knew she weighed a heck of a lot more than that. Jane opened her eyes when he set her down. He moved to pick up a small leather satchel that sloshed with water. He tugged out a seal from the rim and their gazes met as he offered the water satchel to her. Jane's hands were trembling as she gripped the bag and lifted it to her lips. She took a deep drink before handing it back.

The rustling sound of approaching footsteps startled Jane. Her protector jumped up, sword again at the ready, but lowered it when five equally tall, muscle-bound hulks came charging in with their swords drawn. It was all too much for Jane. She felt the blood drain from her face. The world tilted off kilter before fading to black.

~ * ~

She was pure blue fire from the moment he kissed her to the moment she saved his life. The two Drac Scoulls had snuck up on them while he had been pleasantly distracted. She had amazed him by stabbing one of the Drac Scoulls in the back then killed the other with its own sword, no less. Drystan had quickly finished off the one she had wounded. Kell women would have been too delicate for such a deed. They would have simply screamed and begged for their warriors to keep them safe. But no, not this fierce little blue-eyed beauty. Oh, he wanted more of this one and indeed he was going to secure it. With one taste of her sweet, soft lips, lust and desire had inflamed his body, shocking him to his core. One kiss was not going to be enough.

When the warriors returned, it had seemed too much for her. Drystan had watched her pale before collapsing on to his cloak.

"I see you found the Scoulls," Adalardo said, eyeing the two dead bodies. Drystan collected his dagger from the back of the Drac's body. Adalardo crouched down by the girl's side and frowned. "Did you not heal her?"

"Aye, she is merely overwhelmed by her exertions."

Adalardo glanced up at him.

"Exertions, by the Moons of Kell, what did you do to her?"

The other warriors were gathering up the bodies of the Drac to dispose of them. Drystan eyed Adalardo. He didn't like him so close *his* woman.

Drystan stopped himself--the same possessive streak had emerged again. He had saved her. He had kissed her. She had kissed him. She had saved his life. Yes. She *was* his. The war was over. There was no reason for him not to take a mate. He may not know the little beauty lying on his furs, but every basic instinct he possessed told him it was right, that she was right for him. He was going to keep her, no matter what. He looked at the King. He could not make claim to her yet. Not here, not now.

"She killed the Scoull." Drystan was never one to claim another's victory. All the men looked at him in disbelief.

"Surly you jest," Melor said.

"A woman killing?" Briac said with confusion.

Another began, "But how could a girl?"

"With its sword," Drystan cut them off. "She stabbed this one in the back saving my life. Then, when the other attacked her, she slew it with its own sword."

31

The men did not counter his claim as Drystan was always taken at his word. The men stared at her in awe and wonder.

"I guess you owe her a life debt now," Adalardo pointed out.

"Anyone who beheld her would not know how fierce she can be," Drystan mused, collecting his water satchel. He wrapped the girl in his furs and lifted her gently into his arms, carrying her towards his stags.

"I'll take her," the King said. Drystan paused and frowned. He didn't want to release the girl from his arms, but he also didn't want to deny the King in front of the men.

He waited for Adalardo to mount before handing the girl up. He bit back a pang of jealousy as Adalardo wrapped a securing arm around her with her head tucked onto his chest. Drystan tore his gaze away and marched to his stag.

Chapter Four

The air was cooling when they reached Twin Moon Valley. The first moon had already begun to rise which meant darkness would soon descend upon the land.

At first light Drystan would set up a roster of patrols to move from the eastern side of the Blue Mountains down along the path towards to the valley. This was the path the crystal gatherers used. A patrol would offer the workers protection and have a better chance of spotting any Drac in the area. They rounded a bend in the road following the line of the river. Coming to a shallow ford, they crossed through the water, reaching the edge of the outer village.

Many Kell dome-houses in the outer village were empty of inhabitants as the people had moved to the inner township to live under the protection of the Crystal Palace. Anger burned in Drystan that it had proved insufficient in the aftermath of the Drac's vicious raid. In the months that followed, they had worked to improve the townships defenses, swearing to never allow such an assault to happen again.

In the fading light they slowed to a trot as the outer walls of the inner township came into view. Drystan could see men aligning the glow crystals before darkness came. They passed through the heavy stone gate the workers had infused with *Monyo* crystals to help improve its strength.

Men were returning to their homes after the day's labor. They bowed respectfully as the King's stag passed. Drystan saw the look of surprise on their faces when they noticed the King held a woman in his arms. The group turned onto the main path to the Crystal Palace and began the twisting assent. Riding beside the King, Drystan heard the girl give a soft moan. She was starting to wake. Her eyes opened. She glanced around with a panicked look. When her eyes met his, he gave her a reassuring nod, hoping she understood she was safe and to stay calm. She seemed to get the message. Her body stilled and glanced up at Adalardo who smiled warmly down at her. She looked away from the King, a frown creasing her forehead. Drystan noticed her dragging her lower lip through her small teeth in a gesture of worry. Drystan was longing to taste her lips again and draw that soft plump lip through his teeth. Drystan shifted on his stag, attempting to ease the discomfort in his groin, trying to reign in his lusty thoughts and make his cock deflate. It was useless.

The top of her soft, brown head moved about as she glanced around at her surroundings. Her gaze moved up towards the palace, her eyes widening in awe. Drystan struggled to suppress a growl when he watched the King pull her tighter.

"Crystal Palace." Adalardo introduced his home to her. She frowned again, clearly not understanding. There was a communication barrier. Drystan knew some Tell-roc crystal powder under the girl's tongue would solve the language problem. It was a substance used by the scholar class to help them understand a new race's language. It had been a long time since any had been needed.

Reaching the plateau of the palace, the stags trotted across the crystal bridge. Glow crystals lit the entire area of the outer stable yard. Servant boys came running forward to tend to their stags and to any needs of the warriors.

Adalardo dismounted, barking a string of orders. The girl was still sitting on his stag gazing at her surrounding in wonderment. The King reached forward to take hold of her waist in order to lift her off the stag. She jumped on contact, quickly slapping away his hand with a fierce determined stare. Drystan smiled at *his* little Blue Fire. Adalardo frowned. Did she not like being touched? Or was it being touched by the King? The thought pleased Drystan. It was his touch he wanted her to crave.

She seemed understand what Adalardo wanted and swung her right leg over the saddle, slipping easily off the stag's back. Now she was forced to tilt her head back in order to look up at the King as he towered above her. Adalardo smiled, admiring her tenacity, being such a small girl surrounded by tall large men. Drystan strode to them, wanting to be near *his* woman. The girl's blue eyes locked with his. Her cheeks turned a lovely shade of pink before she tore her gaze away.

"Fetch a pouch of Tell-roc crystal. Bring it to the chamber adjacent to mine," Adalardo ordered. Drystan tensed. "Send for Vanora. The girl may feel more at ease with another woman present." Drystan relaxed slightly before nodding. With one more glance at the girl, Drystan pivoted on his heel and strode off. As he walked away, he swore could feel the heat of the girl's gaze on his back.

~ * ~

Jane was definitely in a dream world as the large man who had held her on the weird looking horse led her through a series of long halls, up winding stone steps and into a very large chamber. It looked fit for a King of old medieval earth. Jane glanced up. In the centre of the room, there were rich golden drapes hanging down from a dome ceiling to the floor. Two red velvet sashes held the curtains apart to reveal a large square bed which seemed to dominate the room. The floor beneath her feet was made up of soft, grey stone. There were chairs and tables near the window made from crystal. Jane had never seen so many crystals of every shape and size in all her life. They were everywhere, hanging from the ceiling, giving light in the walls. It was breathtakingly beautiful the way the colors swirled, sparkled, and danced before her eyes. Jane walked to the table where a golden platter, a stark contrast against the crystal table, held an array of strange looking...um, she wasn't sure. Fruit?

Jane was famished. She hadn't eaten all day. Her mouth watered and her stomach grumbled. She reached for what looked like a cross between an apple and a peach but froze mid-reach. She felt eyes watching her. Jane turned. Oh cripes, she'd almost forgotten about him. The leader of the hulks. He seemed to be studying her with great interest, a half smile playing over his lips. She'd better remember her manners and not take anything unless invited.

"I'm kind of hungry. Do you mind if I have one?" She gestured towards the fruit platter, hoping he understood. Jane watched as the large man removed the heavy looking chain from around his chest, along with a jewel-inlaid sword, and laid it upon a large intricately carved chest on

36

the far end of the room. Even though he was disarmed, he was still dangerous. He crossed the floor to stand beside her at the table. Standing a little too close for her comfort, Jane had an urge to step back from him but found some courage and stood her ground. He picked up one of the strange looking fruit.

"*Chan-ra see tall-de trouh.*" His deep rich voice was low with a husky tone. He held out the fruit. She had to step forward in order to take it. What was he trying to do? Seduce her with a piece of fruit? Pe-lease! She smiled, snatched the fruit quickly, and stepped back. She bit down into its flesh giving a small moan of pleasure as the sweet juices ran down her throat. The rest of the fruit didn't last too long under her hungry attentions. The hulk leader chuckled softly before offering her another. She didn't hesitate in taking it. It, too, quickly vanished.

"Oh, so good. What do you call these?" The hulk leader lifted a quizzical eyebrow, making him look more handsome. Jane gave a sigh. It was going to take a long time to learn his language.

Jane remembered something her sister Tamara had once told her about the way she liked her men-- tall, strong and as thick as morning toast. Tamara had dated a lot of foreigners, not all too good with their English. She would love to have seen her sister's face if she hooked up with this muscle-bound hulk. He reached out, running his finger along the side of Jane's face. She jumped back in surprise, bumping against the table. It rocked slightly. Her reaction didn't seem to bother him as he moved in closer.

"Uh look, I don't know what you want from me, but you ain't getting any of that!" When he reached for her again, he was softly tusking with his tongue. *Tusking*! As if he was gently rebuking a naughty child.

Jane slapped his hand away harder this time and shook her head. "No! No touching." Cripes, as if he understood. He looked at her in genuine surprise before he smiled again, unfazed. He wasn't going to give up so easily. He reached out, sifting his fingers through her hair. He cupped the back of her head in his hand to draw her forward. He licked his lips. His gaze was fixed on her mouth. He wanted to kiss her, Jane realized in horror, no not horror… astonishment, delight, excitement, but wait! Who in their right mind would want to kiss her? Kiss Jane Walker.

Jane wanted only one barbarian hulk to kiss her, and he definitely wasn't in the room.

No, no, no, this situation was all too crazy to allow anything as stupid as this to happen. Jane had to take action before he kissed her.

Jane straightened, sucked in a breath, and leaned in closer to him. Oh, he liked that. His other hand moved forward to snake around her waist. Jane had seen this done on TV and hoped it would work on "I-want-to-kiss-you" King of the hulks.

She moved her body to his side, put a leg behind his, and used all her strength to shove him backwards. As he was already partly off balance, his heavy body toppled like a tall tree falling in the forest. Jane tore herself from his grasp as he went down, hitting the floor with a heavy thud. A string of angry sounds sprung from his lips. For a big guy he was quick and was back on his feet before Jane could race towards the door. Her gaze darted about the room, searching for the next best thing. Jane made for his weapon. Drawing his sword, she swivelled around, raising the heavy blade.

"Stay away, you sick bastard!" she hissed. All his features were darker somehow, a muscle ticked in his jaw. No doubt he was angry. She'd tossed him to the ground. She had taken his sword. But she had the right to, didn't she? No one else around here was going to protect Jane but Jane!

~ * ~

Drystan's footsteps pounded through the inner halls of the Palace. He kept a thin measure of control on his anger. He was not usually like this. Drystan was known for his cool composure and self-control. Even on the battle field, he kept a tight rein on his emotions. But today he had found himself on the brink of falling to several emotions which threatened his legendary calm.

His Blue Fire's soft sun-kissed scent had invaded his senses. The way she had felt in his arms, those wide, blue eyes, the way she had kissed him, the way she had fought like a *screel-cat*, slaying one of their enemies. Lust, desire, passion had flared. Oh gods, those lush pink lips. He was desperate with a need to taste them, again and again. Then do oh so much more. An image of the woman, rounded with his child, flashed through is mind. She was his! Rage, jealousy had hit him at the King's sudden possessiveness. Drystan had wanted to rip the woman from Adalardo's arms several times during the journey back to the Crystal Palace and pound his form into the ground.

There was only one cure for his moods, he thought darkly. If the King wanted to make claim to the girl, then Drystan would have to challenge him for her. He knew the ramification of such an action-- whoever won would have to take her as his Protected. This was not a bad prospect, Drystan thought. Unfortunately the loser would be humiliated. This was not a good thing to do to your sovereign and your friend.

Drystan was filled with a sense of urgency as he stormed into the scholar's quarters, demanding the Tell-roc powder, snapping at the servants to find Vanora. He didn't want to leave his Blue Fire with the

King for too long. Would Adalardo hurt her? No, he would not harm her--he could do worse and seduce her away from him.

"*Mine,*" he growled. Vanora, the only female in residence at the Palace, had caught up with him as he passed the great hall, heading for the King's chambers. She was the mother of Briac, a strong warrior and one of his elite. Vanora sadly had lost her daughter in the Drac raid. Briac's sister had been a beautiful, well-rounded lady gracing the courts. She had been promised to another of his warriors.

"What be your need, my lord?" she asked breathlessly.

"The King has need of you in his chambers--we have a guest," he said before stalking away. He was not going to wait for her to keep pace with him. He had to get back to his Blue Fire, his woman.

Drystan stormed rounded the corner. He was close to the King's chambers. There was a sudden loud crash. He heard Adalardo utter a string of curses. Drystan ran the last few paces to the door and flung it open, ready to pounce. But the scene before made him jerk to an abrupt stop.

The woman had somehow managed to take the King's sword, pointing it at him. By the way she held it in her trembling hands, it was obvious she did not know how to use the larger weapon. Drystan relaxed in amusement. Leaning against the door frame, he crossed his arms over his chest. His little Blue Fire had done it again, this time to the King.

"Problems, Sire?" Drystan gave a small chuckle. Adalardo placed his hands on his waist. His gaze darted from Drystan to the girl and back again. Startled by Drystan's appearance at the door, the girl had rounded the weapon in his direction.

Adalardo scowled at him. "What do you want?" he spat out, seeming annoyed at Drystan's intrusion.

"Tell-roc," Drystan reminded him, tossing the pouch of powdered crystal.

"She is a fighter, this one." The King's expression relaxed slightly as he caught the leather pouch.

"I know. What did you do to make her wield your own sword against you?" Drystan glared at his King.

"I...she... humh." The king scowled. "'Tis none of your business. She has my sword." They both looked at her. Drystan tilted his head slightly. The blade was growing heavy in her hands. Her arms lowered the blade to the floor. He couldn't contain another smile at her courage. He unfolded his arms and stepped into the room, looking directly at the King.

"I want to..." Drystan was cut off.

"My lords!" exclaimed a heavy-breathing Vanora. She had raced through the door, looking about in confusion. Her eyes widened with surprise when she spotted the girl.

"By the Moons of Kell, what a small girl." Vanora glided across the floor, not even bothering to look at the sword. "You poor thing. So dirty, oh and you have been hurt. Come, come, do not be afraid. I will take care of you." Vanora easily removed the heavy blade from the girl's hands and placed it back on the chest next to its sheath. She gave a reproachful glare aimed at himself and the King before ushering her away, disappearing with her into the wash chamber. Vanora did not need to be told what to do--she was a mother to the core.

The room felt empty without the girl's presence. Adalardo moved to pick up his discarded sword. He re-sheathed it and placed it safely into his trunk. Drystan focused his attention back on Adalardo and drew in a breath.

"I want to make claim to the girl."

Adalardo's nostrils flared in aggravation. "No, you cannot," he countered.

"Are you making a claim to her then?" Drystan kept his tone steady.

"Are you questioning the intentions of your King?" Adalardo looked as if he was ready to recover his sword to use it against him. Drystan struggled to remain calm at Adalardo's reaction to his claim.

"Yes. If you do not wish to make a claim, then I shall. If you do, then I will challenge it."

"Do you challenge for the throne as well?" Adalardo glared at Drystan. He shook his head.

"I think you know me well enough to understand I have no desire for your throne. I simply want the woman."

Adalardo nodded, his expression softened, and he looked thoughtful for a long moment.

"Then you are aware of the consequences if I do and you lose?"

"Aye."

Adalardo walked across the room to gaze out the darkened window, his back to Drystan, arms clasped behind his back, and his feet apart. It was the stance a warrior used while planning for a battle.

"I did desire the woman for myself. I have the burden of having to produce an heir, Drystan."

The confession did not surprise him. As much as he felt for the heavy burden Adalado had to carry as King, he would have to find another to take as queen.

Adalardo waved his hand. "Very well, my friend." He turned to face him. "As I do not want a woman who is going to try to steal my sword from me every time I try to kiss her, she is yours."

Drystan had to fight to keep his rage in check upon hearing Adalardo had tried to kiss her, but considering how she had reacted, he relaxed somewhat. Relief flooded through Drystan. The woman was his and he had no need to fight his friend for her.

"Remember, we have to take her to Tuathal. If she is the one from another world, then we need her." Drystan nodded.

"I will take care of her."

"I shall have Vanora bring her to your chambers when she is ready. We will need her talking soon." He tossed back the Tell-roc pouch. Drystan felt like he'd just won the greatest victory of all. As he caught the small pouch, he was actually smiling when he left the King's chambers.

Chapter Five

Jane had been shocked by the fact this large, bulky woman was almost the spitting image of her mother, apart from the fact she was a foot taller and seemed to be forty pounds heavier. To protest being ushered into a bathroom bigger than her apartment back home seemed ridiculous. Were all people around here giants?

She never stopped chattering in her strange foreign language. Jane understood through all the gesturing that the lady wanted her to strip out of her dirty clothes and give her a bath. Jane watched as she poured lotions into a huge in-ground tub of steaming water. She certainly was in desperate need of a bath. Her arm was aching from holding the hulks heavy sword for too long. Jane doubted it would have done her much good at any rate. When *her* hulk came bursting though the door, Jane had felt a measure of safety. He had looked thoroughly amused at her poor handling of his leader's sword.

Jane tried to shake the image of his gorgeous grin from her mind-- an impossible task. Instead, Jane let herself be undressed. When they got down to her underwear, Jane realized the woman was staring at her undergarments.

"What, you never seen panties or bra before?" From the older woman's expression, no. Her face lit in a wide grin as if the concept was a new and brilliant idea. It had certainly stopped her chattering for a moment. She paused. Facing Jane, she placed her hand on her chest.

"Vanora." Recognition dawned--she was introducing herself. At last someone was talking to her, not at her or over her.

"Vanora," Jane acknowledged, smiling before touching her own chest to introduce herself. "Jane."

"Jane," Vanora repeated with a smile. Then she launched into another string of chattering as she ushered Jane towards the bath, holding up a towel to help ease her modesty. Jane accepted gratefully. Vanora was the mother of some proud son or daughter, no doubt.

Jane finished stripping as Vanora gathered up her clothing and hurried out, leaving Jane to climb into the marbled bath tub. She sank into the warm water then let out a soft sigh of pleasure. The heat of the water felt so good against her skin. Jane tensed, thinking about the two huge barbarian hulks in the other room. Jane though it best not to linger too long, lest they come in search of her, finding her naked in a bath tub. Hummm, that gorgeous man, the way he had felt, the way he had kissed her. She closed her eyes for a moment, recalling it.

"Oh, for heaven's sake," she muttered, snapping her eyes open. It was probably just a one off thing. Jane was not the type of woman huge good-looking men went for. They wanted young, pretty, skinny women with big breasts. At least Jane qualified in one area, she mused dryly. No, it was just a fluke. Despite the strange place she now found herself, men were men.

She hurriedly washed herself before climbing up out of the bath, grabbing the bath sheet and rubbing her body dry. The soft grey towel was so large it wrapped around her twice.

Vanora burst back though the door, holding new clothes. Jane stared at the fabric. Whatever it was, it looked miles too big, not to mention she had no idea how to put it on.

She gave Vanora a *'please help me'* look. She seemed to understand. With a motherly smile, she demonstrated how the top lay across her back, crossing over her breasts, and tied up at the back.

The silken fabric shimmered blue with swirling multi-pastel colors. It was beautiful. Jane was accustomed to wearing simple jeans, t-shirts, and jumpers. Jane tried to recall the last time she wore something this nice. She failed.

Vanora helped her pull it up around her shoulders. It hooked across her breasts to provide a plunging neckline, revealing the swell of her breasts before wrapping around her waist and lower legs. The skirt hung down with two large splits on either side, revealing her legs and lower part of her thighs each time she took a step. The outfit hugged her body, revealing every ugly bulge. Jane frowned. But Vanora's dark eyes gleamed with approval.

Jane felt uncomfortable and vulnerable as if she was being prepared for a feast, with her as the main course.

Vanora ran a comb though Jane's hair and helped her with some black sandals before guiding her back into the large bed chamber, which was blessedly free of occupants, and straight out to the exit.

Jane needed to try and communicate with these people. So far, dealing with the hulks had a few undesirable results. Maybe she could try to get through to Vanora instead. She needed to find out where she was, how she got here, but more importantly, how to get home.

They had been walking, turning, and twisting through long halls. Jane followed Vanora down a few flights of stairs. Jane had no idea where they were going. Stopping at a door, Vanora opened it and Jane followed her through. Vanora gave her a reassuring pat on the arm before walking out and closing the door behind her.

Cripes! Where was she now? There was another huge four poster bed with dark purple coverings. Rich red drapes hung from the ceiling very much like the first chamber she had been in. A long dark grey rug covered a good portion of the floor. She saw a plain wooden table with two chairs situated near the door where she had entered. The table was dressed with a black table cloth . On top of that was a large platter laden with breads, meats, and few other things she could not identify. A golden jug and two goblets also adorned the table. A strange little black leather pouch was set off to one side and seemed out of place.

Two place settings tipped Jane off to the fact that this room wasn't just for her use. Jane noticed several large trunks lined up in a row along the wall next to a second door. And a huge rectangular mirror hung off the wall. If this chamber was anything like the layout of the other chamber, then the second door led to a bathroom. But something else caught Jane's attention. Furs. A fur cloak. Jane padded silently over to them, running her fingers though the plush pile. She lifted them to her nose and inhaled. The heady masculine scent immediately sent a wave of heat through her body. She knew who these belonged to. It then dawned on her whose room this was. The second door opened and in he stepped.

Jane's jaw dropped, her mouth went dry, her breath caught in her throat. Holy moly! His skin was all bronzed and sexy, large arms rippled with muscles. Lord what strength! His stomach muscles formed a v that pointed down. Her eyes lowered to where the towel covered his hips and legs. Jane's eyes were riveted to a droplet of water trickling down his large sculptured chest.

His dark eyes spotted her, and a seductive smile spread across his face. Jane's knees went weak, forcing her to lean against the chest for support. She dropped the furs in her hand. He strode right past her to the table, picking up the brown leather pouch. He turned, crooked a single finger, beckoning her to come to him. Jane wanted to run up, throw herself into his strong arms, and beg him to do whatever he wanted with her. But the sane, rational Jane stood there gaping and shaking her head. He didn't bother to do it again but stalked forward. Jane tried to back up but had nowhere to go. He shook his head, giving her a look she didn't quite know how to interpret. Was it apologetic?

In a quick movement he grabbed her upper arms and lifted her off her feet. A scream caught in Jane's throat as he carried her towards the bed. When he tossed her down, her legs hung over the side. Jane kicked towards his groin, desperately trying to remember her self-defense lessons. He was quicker, anticipating what she might do. He was on top of her in another instant, straddling her waist, his massive body holding her down. He caught hold of her hands, pinning them down under his knees. The only thing that separated his naked flesh from her was the towel. Jane was quick to realize that struggling was futile. She was helpless against his pure, brute strength. She looked up into the depths of his dark eyes. Was he going to rape her? Jane doubted it would be much of a rape--one kiss from him she would be a willing partner in her ravishment.

No, he delicately opened the little pouch in his hand and stuck his finger in. When he pulled it out, it was covered in a white powder. Oh god, he was going to poison her. She renewed her struggles, thrashing her head as his finger descended to her mouth. No, no, *nononono!* As much as she tried to avoid it, he caught her chin in his large hands and forced her mouth open. In a quick motion he placed the powder under her tongue. Then released her from his grasp and backed off the bed.

Saliva melted with the powder, forcing Jane to swallow. Her entire mouth tingled. It was like a current of electricity shooting right through to her brain. Jane groaned, rolled over, and gripped the sides of her head. What on Earth had he given her?

"*Perr-ta,* little Blue Fire," she heard his rich husky voice. "Blue Fire *kerr- trum,* it was necessary."

Jane blinked. Had he just spoken English? She sat up. Her head was throbbing.

"What did you give me?" She glared at him.

"Tell-roc Crystal," he moved in closer. "You hear my words now?"

Jane nodded, dumbfounded.

"My apologies for the manner in which I had to distribute it. It helps us understand each other. I guessed you would assume it was poison and would not have taken it willingly."

He had assumed right. "My head hurts."

He fetched a goblet and poured liquid into it before handing it to her. Gratefully, she took the cup and drained it of its delicious, fruity wine.

"It will pass soon." He took the empty goblet from her.

Jane was finding it hard to think clearly, her eyes fixating on his mammoth, rippling chest.

"I um… I," she stammered like an idiot. "Will you *please* put some clothes on?"

"You do not like what you see, Blue Fire?"

49

Jane was startled by the wicked gleam in his eyes and his suggestive tone.

"Yes, I mean no. I mean it's distracting!"

"I could say the same for you." His gaze swept over her.

She was half raised off the bed, resting on her arms, with her legs parted. The material of the skirt had ridden up, revealing her pale legs right up to the junction of her thighs.

Jane felt her cheeks heat and scrambled to cover herself. He gave a rich husky chuckle, sending shivers down her spine.

"Well, at least I'm wearing clothes," she protested, pointing her finger at his chest. "You're not!" Shrugging, he turned away from her.

"As you wish."

Oh my god! The thought flashed through Jane's brain as she was treated to a view of his broad, bare back and shoulders. She wanted to run her fingers over them and feel his skin under her palms. When he tugged a shirt over his head, Jane sagged in disappointment--her eye candy had been covered. She climbed off the bed, desperately needing to get her focus off Mr. Body for a moment.

Think, think, think, stupid. She tapped the side of her head with her palm. She heard rustling of more clothing. No, no, no she would not look. But her imagination had already seen his round, naked ass, his legs strong as tree trunks, and his... oooh... she gulped. Manhood.

Focus!

"Where am I and who are you?" There, a sensible question for Mr. Hunky. Jane sat down on one of the chairs.

"I am Drystan, Commander of the King's Warriors. You, little Blue Fire, are in the Land of the Kell. This," he swept his hand in front of him, "is the Crystal Palace and my chambers."

"Well, that much I figured out," was her dry response. In a few strides of his long legs, he seated himself on the chair opposite. It creaked in protest under his weight. "Kell, never heard of it. And I know for a fact there are no warriors on Earth any more. They belong in storybooks and the pages of history."

"This Earth is your land? Is it abundant of people like you?"

"Like me? As in human?"

"As in lovely, blue-eyed women."

Jane thought the question odd and answered in a roundabout way.

"Hobart-that's where I live. There are about two hundred thousand people and plenty of women. And they have different colored eyes." She frowned, chewing on her lower lip. "How did I get here, to Kell?"

"You should tell me, Blue Fire." Why the heck was he calling her that? Was it a term of endearment perhaps? No, that was stupid.

"Jane, my name is Jane Walker."

"Jane Walker." He repeated her name like a soft caress. Oh cripes, it sent shivers down Jane's spine.

"Tell me what you remember."

Jane thought back to the cottage cleaning job.

"I had a job, a good one too, up in the mountains. But at the end of the day, I was too tired to drive home. I decided to camp for the night."

"On your own?" He seemed genuinely surprised.

"Well, yes, on my own."

"Have you no protector?"

"Protector?" Jane snorted, "Please, Tasmania may have a lot of wilderness but nothing we need protecting from."

51

"Who cares for your needs? Do you not have suitors?" He pressed.

"I take care of myself, and no, I don't have any *suitors.*" Cripes, a Dark Ages man with a Dark Ages mentality. But a small smile was playing on his lips which made Jane uneasy.

"Continue your story."

Jane drew in a breath and did as he asked.

"Long story short, I slipped and fell into a cave when I went to fetch water. I don't remember much after that. Well, until you." She gestured at him with her hand.

"From what I know, and it is little, you have fallen though a portal or gateway between worlds. You found the one which connects yours to mine."

"I'm on a different world?"

"Aye."

"Then I can go home again?" Jane sat up with hope.

"We have a Sorcerer here in Kell. He told us the journeys though portals are hazardous with no way back."

Jane's shoulders sagged. Her head spun trying to take in the concept of portals and sorcerers.

"Holy crap, I'm on an alien planet!" she verbalized her thoughts. These people didn't look like they had space aged technology. Portals and magic seemed the way to travel from planet to planet. Ether she just proved the theory or she was still having a nightmare.

"Take heart, your arrival here is not unwelcomed. In certitude it is of very great value and importance."

She didn't believe it and shook her head to show her disapproval. "I don't know who you think I am, but I am no one special, I'm just...just Plain Jane."

Drystan frowned at her as if he disapproved of her words.

"Nay, I do not accept such a thing. From the time in the forest when you summoned me forth to kiss you, I knew you were uncommon." Jane felt the heat rising into her cheeks.

"That was a mistake," she blurted out.

He simply raised a dark eyebrow at her. "'Twas no mistake to me."

"I thought I was dreaming, and you were, well, you were not real."

"Mayhap, but I can reassure you here and now how real I am, my Blue Fire."

His black eyes gleamed with a dark fire of their own. He moved swiftly out of his chair, rounded the table, and took hold of her upper arms. Jane gasped in as he hauled her against his massive, hard chest. White-hot jolts of desire shot though Jane on contact, a moan caught in her throat as her head tipped back to look up at him. He lowered his head close to hers. Jane was trembling as he slipped his arm around her waist, to tug her tighter against him. The feel of his warm breath was intoxicating.

"You are no longer without a protector, my Blue Fire Jane." His wine-rich husky tone dipped lower. She shivered.

"No, I...Don't think..." she stammered, her brain turning to mush.

"No thinking," he ordered. "Feel, just feel. You tempted me once with your taste." His lips tentatively brushed against hers. "I have been craving for more. Needing more of you."

Oh god, Jane was utterly lost. This stunning example of male perfection was going to kiss her again. But did he truly desire her? No man in all her existence had ever paid her the slightest bit of attention. But in the heat of the moment, Jane didn't care. She wanted his kisses, and she wanted him to ravish her.

Melting into his arms, she allowed her lashes to flutter closed, surrendering. White-hot desire raced to every part of her body, her nipples hardened, moisture pooling between her legs. He traced his tongue around her lips.

"Open."

Jane obeyed. His tongue was delving inside. Her tongue moved forward before darting back in shy retreat. His hand raked up into her hair to grip her head, controlling the angle of the kiss, plunging his tongue deeper, over and over again. Jane was alive with a desperate hungry need. Their teeth clashed when he bit down on Jane's lower lip. She whimpered, greedy for more.

Chapter Six

Yes, so much better than he remembered. His little wild Blue Fire was in his arms, her body melting against his. Drystan was sublimely aroused. He had been unable to make his cock behave ever since that first kiss in the forest. But seeing her in a lovely feminine Kell dress hugging her every curve, he had battled with himself not to take her right there and then. He knew their talking was necessary, but he had been itching to hold, touch, and taste her. He was determined to kiss and lick every measure of her delicious creamy skin. He lifted her easily, something he could have never done with a Kell woman. Her arms wound up around his shoulders. He felt her fingers slide into his hair, her legs wrapping around his waist. Her soft form against his hardened one seemed to fit perfectly into him. This was a new wonder to have a woman wrap around him like this. The height and largeness of the Kell women made such manoeuvres simply impossible. There was much to explore with his little Blue Fire. The scent of her arousal was enthralling. He backed them to the bed, lowering her down. Without breaking contact, he nibbled and licked a path down her chin and to her neck. She tilted her head back to give him better access to her skin as she ran her hands over his shoulders.

"Strong." She murmured breathlessly. "So strong."

He slid one hand up to the curve of her waist before moving it higher to her breast, feeling the full round globe in his hand, her tight nipple abrading against his palm through the fabric of her dress. Her breasts were perfect for filling his hands. He growled at the barrier of the fabric. He heard her gasp as he pulled the fabric down, freeing the first of her glorious creamy breasts. It had a hard dusty pink nipple which begged to be tasted. When he flicked his tongue over the nipple, it hardened further. She moaned. He sucked it into his mouth, sucking, rolling his tongue around the bud before scraping it with his teeth. Her back arched as if she was offering him more.

"Like?"

"Huh? Oh yes, yes like. More." She breathed in a shuddering breath. He exposed the other creamy breast to give it the same treatment. Then he went back to do it all over again, revelling in the taste of her skin. He moved his hand back down her waist over her outer thighs, stroking her before moving inward across the soft skin and under her skirt. Drystan groaned, hardening almost to the point of pain as he ran his fingers through soft, silky curls between the junction of her thighs. She jumped under him at the contact, sank down into her hot, wet core, as he gently circled the outer rim, rubbing the little nub. She stiffened before relaxing into him. Aahh, yes. Surrender.

A pounding on his door shook Drystan out of his haze. He cursed, hoping whoever it was would go away. But they pounded again. Very reluctantly, he pulled away from his wild Blue Fire. She opened her eyes looking rather dazed and confused. Oh, what a sight he beheld, her flushed skin, her breasts exposed, her soft thighs parted, and her lips swollen from his kisses.

"I shall be back, my sweet." He kissed her lips. "Stay just as you are," he ordered into her mouth. Then he got off the bed, drawing closed the drapes. Only he would ever be privileged to see his Jane like this. He marched to the door and yanked it open to glare at the one who dared intrude.

"What be it?" he barked. The servant blanched under his fierceness.

"The King, Commander, he wishes your presence in the Great Hall." The man stepped back. The King lacked in timing, Drystan thought darkly.

"I shall be there presently," he told the servant before slamming the door shut. He pivoted on his heel, marched back to the bed and ripped open the curtains. Jane had not obeyed him, but had moved back to the head-board, covering herself and sitting with her legs drawn up. Fire and passion one moment, the next looking like frightened prey. He gave a heavy sigh.

"I must attend to the King. You will stay here. Eat, rest, regain your strength, my Blue Fire Jane." He flashed a smile of intent. "You shall need it when I return." He was satisfied when she nodded, but was uneasy she did not say anything. He could see the heat from their passion still burning in her cheeks. He turned away from her, heading back out the door.

Soon, he promised himself as he strode down the hall. Soon he would have her completely.

~ * ~

Jane jumped off the bed as soon as the door closed. Oh god, she was a first class idiot. She had let a stranger, and an alien, seduce her. Oh, but it had felt so good. Was she so starved of touch and affection, she drank down every drop of attention like a woman dying of thirst? She was still turned on and almost felt like finishing herself off in order to get some relief.

Jane forced herself to pause to think about her situation. The fact was that she was the alien in a strange land. They had black hair, black eyes, dark features. She had blue eyes, brown hair, and pale skin. He must see her as something exotic compared to what he was used to. Maybe Drystan was some kind of Captain Kirk flying around in his starship tying to sex up any exotic alien female that crossed his path. Yet Drystan, commander of the King's Warriors, was nothing like Captain Kirk.

"Oh god, oh god," she repeated over and over as she paced the room. She had to get out of here. Jane felt her stomach rumbled and realized how hungry she was.

"Eat, rest, regain your strength," he had ordered. She would at least obey part of his direction. She sat down and began to stuff her face with the food that had been laid out.

Jane knew the way her body had responded to him. She stood on dangerous ground and was way out of her depth around Drystan. She still tingled from his touch where his tongue had licked and traced over her skin. It was like a shot of heroin. Jane shuddered. How could one man or alien affect her like this? She had come so close to giving him everything she was.

If she stayed, she'd presumably end up as his personal sex slave until he grew bored of her.

"No, not going to happen," she mumbled between bites. Jane polished off more than half the platter of food then scolded herself for eating too much. But then, she didn't know when she was going to get another chance to eat. One good thing out of this, she mused dryly, she'd probably lost another few pounds from lack of food and over-exercise.

She glanced back around the room, her gaze falling on the row of trunks. She had to get out of the 'native' dress she wore. To draw attention was the last thing anyone would want while trying to escape.

Jane walked over to the first trunk. When it refused to open, she tried the next. It was also locked. The third one opened. Bingo. Clothes. Drystan's Clothes. She pulled them out, tossing them behind her until she found what she wanted: a black long sleeve shirt, belt and leather-type pants. She unwound the Kell dress, tossing it into the trunk and pulled on the shirt and pants, securing the two together with the belt. Everything was over sized on her. Winding up the pants legs till she found her feet and making large cuffs on the sleeves, Jane glanced at herself in the mirror. She reached up to touch her hair. They all seemed to have black hair. She had pale brown. She looked back down into the trunk then around at the clothes scattered at her feet. When there was nothing to use, her eyes scanned the room. She gave a grin and hurried over to the table. She lifted the platter, snatching off the table cloth to wrap it around her head and shoulders. Jane examined herself in the mirror; she looked like a baggy scruff. Perfect.

Jane raced to the door, hauling it open. She looked right then left. It was clear of people. Trusting her intuition, Jane went left. Keeping to the shadows between the rows of glowing crystals, she moved quickly.

She turned a right corner and headed down a flight of stairs. Jane's sense of direction was lousy. It didn't matter. She needed only one direction. Out.

~ * ~

Drystan strode into the Grand Hall in a dark, sullen mood. The servants were busy laying the long table with prepared foods. Adalardo sat at the head of the table. Drystan marched the length of the table to sit at Adalardo's right. His mood did not go unnoticed.

"The wild one pull a sword on you too, my friend?" Amusement sparkled in the King's eyes.

"Nay," he snapped harsher than he'd intended. "Interrupted."

The King leaned back with a smile.

"You should be thankful I gave her to you. She did indeed look tempting." The King's tone was wistful. Drystan held back his possessive rage, placated by the fact the King had relented and had given Jane to him, which kept him from knocking him to the ground and beating him into a bloody pulp. King or not. "Matters of state come before pleasure, my friend."

Drystan nodded.

"What have you learned from our little guest?"

The fact she tasted minty feminine. Her skin's flavor was salty and sun-drenched. Her breasts were round and creamy, perfect for filling his hands. He had learned her nipples were delicious to suck on, to toy with. Drystan shifted uncomfortably--he wanted to be back in his chambers doing exactly that. He cleared his throat.

"Her name is Jane Walker, and her land is one called Earth. The city in which she dwelt has a great multitude of people, and many, many women."

"This is good news." Adalardo picked up the goblet, motioning for one of the servants to fill it. A younger, adolescent boy rushed forward to obey. "We shall take her to Tuathal after dawn break." The King lifted the goblet to his lips, drinking deeply. "Have you given her a bracelet yet?"

Drystan had been too absorbed in Jane to put his claim formally upon her.

"I shall soon."

"Do not hesitate too long, lest someone else catches sight of her and challenges your claim." The King was right. In a Kingdom full of men deprived of women, she would be leapt upon in an instant. But she was safely hidden in his chambers, he assured himself. No one dare take her from there.

"This is cause for a celebration of hope, my friend." Men had started to arrive in the hall for their evening meal.

"I beg your leave, Sire." Drystan had a different meal in mind for his supper. The King nodded.

"Do not tire the girl out too much." Adalardo gave a knowing smile. Drystan pushed to his feet, swiftly exiting the hall. He hurried, wanting to be back in his chambers as quickly as possible.

Drystan pondered what she would be doing. Eagerly waiting his return on his bed? Eating? Resting? Even bathing? The thought of water droplets running down her creamy skin, slick, wet, hardened him even more.

What Drystan found made the pit of his stomach drop. Clothes were flung about the chamber, and there was no Jane to be found. Had someone taken her? Drystan shook his head. She was a wild fire. She would have run. Drystan headed back down the halls to search. He had to find her, quickly.

~ * ~

The low laughter of men came from a room just off to Jane's right. Oh crikey, she had been walking around these corridors for what seemed hours now, getting nowhere. Across the far end of the room she spotted a door that seemed to lead into the darkness of the night. It couldn't be the only way out, could it? There were eight strapping strong hulks, most likely some of Drystan's warriors, sitting around a large rectangular table, eating, with huge sharp-looking knives. She couldn't go through there. She needed to backtrack and find a different path.

"What are you doing, boy?" A deep baritone voice from behind her made Jane jump in fright and spin round.

"Nothing, I..." She dared not look up at him. Her blue eyes would give her away. She tried to think of something to say which wouldn't make him suspicious. "Just running errands," she said, lowering the timber of her voice. Then she moved to dart around him, but he clamped a hand down on her shoulder. Jane bit down on her lower lip to stop herself from whimpering in pain.

"What do you have on your head? I know we lack women, but it does not mean you can start acting foolishly." There was amusement in his voice. He reached for her head covering.

"No!" she cried, yanking herself free from his grip. "It's not foolish it's just...just..."

"Saraid, stop tormenting the servants." Another man rounded the corner.

"The boy wears a woman's head covering," the one called Saraid defended. "I was not tormenting."

Jane was cornered. Unless one of them moved she had nowhere to go.

"Many have taken to carrying memories of what they have lost. Boys, servants, even some warriors." Curiosity replaced Jane's fear of discovery. What had they lost?

"He should not be wearing it on his head, Anyon!" They were now facing each other. Jane tried to slip past them but was grabbed, propelled forward into the room full of men. They all looked, turning their attention to her. She gulped, keeping her gaze low.

"Was it your mother's, boy?" Saraid asked.

Jane nodded trying to keep up the ploy.

"Look at me!" he snapped angrily. Jane shook her head.

"Saraid," growled Anyon in a warning. "Leave him be."

"Not till he acts like a man."

"Here we go," another said with sarcasm.

Her covering was then yanked off. The game was up. There was a collective gasp. Then another when she glanced up, revealing her eye color. Jane jumped, using the moment of surprise to kick Saraid in the shin, hard. It hurt her toes but achieved the desired result. He bent down to grab at his leg. At that moment, she thrust her hand forward, her palm colliding on his nose with a crack. He released her, cussing in pain. She darted from the room as fast as her feet could carry her.

She never even reached the corridor. She was grabbed from behind, lifted, carried back and dumped on the table.

"It's a girl," one exclaimed with undeniable excitement.

"Never have I seen blue eyes before," one of the men said.

"She's very small." They encircled her.

"Looks like a little *Qell* has stumbled into a *Breven* den," another chuckled.

"Pretty hair." One reached out to feel it in his fingers.

"No touching," Jane growled at them, "or I'll cut your hand off!" She slapped him away.

"She broke my nose!" Blood trickled to his mouth. Saraid was also rubbing his shin. "It is not a woman, it is a harpy!"

"You have had worse, Saraid, grow up," someone told him.

"I'll do a lot more than break your nose if you touch me," she hissed. They all looked at her with a mix of surprise and delight before chuckling.

"I like taming wild things," one said.

"From where have you come?" the one called Anyon questioned.

"From the third star on the right and straight on till morning." The joke was on her as none of them understood the Peter Pan reference.

"A fallen star." He smiled at her.

"What be your name, Little Star?"

"Why was she running around the palace?" Saraid interrupted. He had a cloth of material pressed against his nose, wiping up the blood.

"My name is Jane, and I am lost. I need to go home." She told them the exact truth.

"Do you grant wishes, Little Star Jane?"

"I wish for a kiss," one of the men said. They all chuckled.

"No wishes, no kisses," she informed them, bravely raising her chin.

"Never mind them," Anyon said. "It's just been too long since we have had such lovely company. They have forgotten their manners."

"Are you not married?" Jane asked them. "Surly strong handsome men as yourselves have devoted ladies?" A look of sad anguish crossed their faces.

"She is from another world. She does not know."

"What don't I know?"

"They were all murdered, Little Star, by our enemy the Drac."

Jane gasped, her heart felt for them.

"I am truly sorry for your loss," she said softly. "How could such a thing happen?" Jane wanted to understand. "Please tell me." Some of the men sat down as Anyon told the story of the war, the battle, the surprise attack. After they were all silent, she could see they all blamed themselves.

"Where I am from," Jane broke the silence, "the women are not all helpless, some are strong warriors. We are brave. We go wherever we like, do whatever we like and without fear."

They all looked at her with great interest.

"A woman's place is in her man's bed, not wandering about." It was Saraid who spoke.

"Well, if your woman was out learning how to fight, she'd still be here now," Jane snapped. He jumped from his chair with rage in his eyes.

"How dare you!"

"Saraid!" Anyon grabbed him. She had said the wrong thing. These men were hurting.

"I am sorry. My words were thoughtless," she apologized, smiling softly at him. He nodded, relaxing. "Let us just say, things are as they are in my land and in your land."

They all agreed. "You fellows are being terrible hosts. You have yet to offer me anything to drink or eat." She smiled as they scrambled to attend to her wants. Jane watched in amusement as the men tripped over themselves to play doting hosts.

"I like this." She held the fruity wine in a crystal goblet. "What do you call it?"

"Kell wine."

Jane grinned. "How dull. In my land our men are like wine."

"Why is that?" Anyon asked.

"They all start out like fruit. It's the women's job to stomp on them and keep them in the dark until they mature into something with which you'd like to have dinner." There was a pregnant pause before the entire room erupted with laughter. Jane giggled.

"I like this girl, as skinny as she may be."

Jane laughed at his comment. "You're a funny man," she told him. "In my land the more slim and petite you are, the more you are deemed attractive." They all looked shocked.

"Surely not? Little star, in Kell, the larger the lady, the more she is desired." It was Jane's turn to be surprised.

"But I say you would be a nice size for me." Anyon gave her a look, making her nervous. Jane shrugged, trying to make light of his comment.

"Well boys, it's been lovely meeting you, but I must be going." She stood up.

"Little Star, there is something else you should know about our customs." Anyon glanced at the other men.

"If a girl is of age and allowed to wander free, any man has right to make a claim on her, to be her Protector."

A sudden fear shot though Jane. She hid it by trying to look disinterested. But she had heard those words before. Drystan had said something about her protecting. She suddenly wanted his protection when faced with the hungry looks these men were giving her. Jane resolved not to let them get the better of her.

66

"I saw her first," Saraid jumped in. Jane groaned.

"You will stop such talk at once!" Jane snapped. "I do not want a protector, nor do I need one."

"You are in Kell, you must," Saraid countered.

"We need women here. You are as womanly as I have ever seen, even in turrets." Anyon was about to reach out to touch her.

"The woman belongs to me!" They all jumped at the sound of a deep, angry voice-one which Jane recognized. Drystan was standing in the door, arms crossed over his chest, and a dark scowl on his face as he glared at the men. "Back off now or I will have each one of you skewered to a spiral spike and put out front of the palace on display." Jane felt the blood drain from her face. They all backed away from her as if she was diseased.

"Commander, we did not know, and she did not say," Saraid stammered.

"Silence!" he barked. "You are all on the first mountain patrol before dawn break." His eyes were like a black storm of jealousy and rage as they looked at her. He strode into the room, taking hold of her wrist and pulling her out. Jane was too frightened to protest, even with the warm tingles moving though her arm.

"Drystan, let me go." She tried to yank herself free. He did not relent, marching her back though the corridors.

"Do you realize how much jeopardy you put yourself in by leaving my chambers?" he growled.

"I just wanted to go home." Jane winced as her voice sounded like a whining child. "Drystan, you're hurting me!" He released her wrist. Rounding on her, he backed her against the wall. Gently he lifted her wrist and kissed her where he had gripped her to tightly. God, his sudden changes of moods were giving her whiplash.

67

"Jane, Jane," he chided softly. "Hurting you is not my intention." Her body heated at the touch of his lips on her skin.

"Do not touch me, I...I don't want to be touched by you!" she blurted out. He stepped back, dropping her hand. His gaze roamed over her from head to toe.

"Did any of my warriors touch you?" Although his voice was calm, the rage in his eyes was evident.

"Well, Saraid tried but I broke his nose," she said, hoping the knowledge would appease Drystan.

"You broke one of my warrior's noses?" His lips twitched up at the corners in amusement.

"Yes, the others were nice to me." She had to come to their defense. Jane felt Drystan would carry out his earlier threat of putting their heads on spikes. "They told me what happened to the women of Kell." The look in Drystan's eyes changed again. Jane could almost feel his anguish and guilt.

"I cannot even begin to understand. I'm sorry for what you have gone through. It must be hard," she said softly, genuinely wishing there was something she could do to help these people.

"Then please understand this, Jane. You can help us. Help the people of Kell have a future."

Jane was confused. "I am no one special. I'm just a plain ordinary woman, Drystan. I don't see what I could possibly do to help."

"In the morning we will see the sorcerer, Tuathal. He will tell us. You, Jane, are the key to it all."

Jane blinked in disbelief at his words, wondering when she would wake up. Kings, drop dead gorgeous Warriors, Sorcerers, and Crystals. All Jane needed now was a dragon to top it off. The old movie saying, "*Toto, I don't think we're in Kansas anymore,*" seemed to apply here. "Come back to my chambers now. We need to rest before the 'morrow. Before our future and fate is decided." He offered his hand to her. Jane gave a sigh and relented, placing her hand into his.

He walked her back through the corridors to his chambers. She sat down by the table. Jane noticed that someone had come in and cleaned up the mess she had made earlier. Her shoulders sagged, suddenly feeling very tired. She watched him stride over to the first of his trunks. Unlocking it, he removed something small before returning to stand in front of her.

"I want you to wear this." In his palm he held a lovely golden bracelet. With a little heart shaped lock. Holding the two halves together, he unlocked it with a small key. Eyeing him with suspicion, Jane wondered why he would give her jewellery.

"It's beautiful, but I can't accept such a thing."

This man did not like having to repeat himself. He simply seized her right wrist and snapped it around, re-locking it. It was a little loose, but she could not get it off.

"You will." There was finality to his words which set Jane on edge.

"What is it?"

"'Tis a promise bracelet. It will protect you from other men." Jane felt she was living in a perpetual state of confusion with all the new things Drystan told her.

"How?"

"'Tis my claim on you. You, Jane Walker, belong to me now. I am your Protector." Jane blinked as she realized what he meant. Jane's temper flared and she jumped to her feet.

"Oh, no, no, no. Take it off this instant." She tried tugging it over her hand. The thing was too small. It would not go.

"Drystan, I will not belong to anyone, especially you! I am not, not property!" Her voice level had risen. She had felt her cheeks flame red in anger and frustration.

"So you would prefer me to give you to Anyon or Saraid?"

"I'm not anyone's to give!" Jane refused to back down. "You're...you're an intimidating bully. And I won't have it. I won't have you!"

He just smiled at her.

Grrrr! In all her life she had never known such a frustrating man! She stomped her foot.

"Enough," he said. "Bed. You must rest now. Tomorrow will be a long day."

"No friggen way am I sleeping here with you," she said, folding her arms across her chest. How dare he do this to her.

"Are all Earth women as stubborn as you?" he asked, seemingly undaunted by her outburst of temper.

"Oh, matey, you have nooo idea. We are stubborn, headstrong, fiery. We are not mild, meek or subservient."

"Then I shall delight in teaching you the error of your ways. The way a woman should be to her man." Jane rolled her eyes, groaning in frustration at his arrogance. But the exhaustion of the day was beginning to get to her. So much had happened. All Jane wanted to do was sleep. Keeping her pride intact, there was no way she was going to stay in the same room as Drystan or she'd never get any sleep tonight.

"I will not sleep on that bed. And I will not sleep with you." She waved her finger at him. He gave a casual shrug.

"I think you shall miss my warmth, Jane. And the untold pleasures I can give you." He gave her a seductive smile. Jane swallowed hard, having already tasted some of the pleasure Drystan could give her. She fought against her traitorous body, screaming to throw herself back into his arms, beg him to finish what he'd started earlier that evening. Drystan sat down on the bed, giving the bed cover an inviting pat to beckon her forth. "But I shall sleep here."

Jane glared at him, hands on her hips as she glanced around the room weighing her options. She searched for a place to sleep. She wasn't going to give him the satisfaction of giving in. Jane marched into the bathroom and slammed the door. Here would do just fine.

Chapter Seven

She was such a stubborn woman. He could hear her pacing back and forth in the wash room, muttering aloud. "Stupid arrogant men, nothing but male chauvinist pigs, never heard of women's rights. How dare he do this to me!"

Drystan lay on his bed, far from tired, his body still aching with need. He longed to march into the wash chamber, rip off her clothes, and swallow her protests with his mouth before sinking himself between her soft, creamy thighs. He needed release or would never get any rest this night. He would not take it out on Jane. No, he wanted her soft and willing. She needed to recognize her own body's needs and surrender to him freely.

Drystan jerked himself to the edge of the bed before releasing the top of his turrets. He groaned as his hard, thick cock swung free. He would simply have to take matters into his own hands. He gripped his cock, squeezing at the base, before sliding up to his sensitive tip. Closing his eyes, he imagined Jane's hand soft around his width. He pumped up and down, seeing her lovely, plump breasts, beautiful nipples drawn into hard berries, aching for him to touch and taste them. He pondered what her sweet mouth would feel like on his cock, hot, wet, and oh so sweet. Her tongue would swipe along his slit before licking down the underside. Drystan collected his weeping pre-cum at the tip to lubricate as he pumped his hand harder and faster, tugging, pulling. It did not take long to feel the first pulls of his release. Drystan groaned deeply, his hand pumping in short jerks until his seed spilled out onto the floor. He let his breathing calm before pushing to his feet. It was no substitute for Jane, but it would do for now. He would only be truly sated once he had his Blue Fire. Even then he doubted he would ever get enough of her. Normally he would do this in the wash chamber, but it was occupied...He needed a towel to clean up the floor. Tucking his cock back in, he fastened his turrets and headed into the wash chamber. He braced himself for the string of verbal insults she would hurl. Surprisingly he was greeted with silence. Glancing around, he spotted her asleep on a pile of towels and clothes in the corner of the chamber. Her pale, brown hair splayed over a dark, makeshift pillow.

She had called herself plain. Why did she think herself unattractive? Surely she had seen his desire for her. What kind of a world had she come from where women were devalued thus? He knelt down, brushing a few strands of hair from her face. The simple contact brought warmth to his skin. He was amazed at how this small woman could affect him so deeply.

Self-loathing was something impregnated from childhood, drummed, beaten into a person. He would like to get his hands on the ones responsible for his woman's poor self image. Drystan wanted to see her shine like the jewel she was. He had seen such strength of spirit. It was his duty as her Protector to draw out her full potential.

He scooped her up in his arms. She stirred momentarily to nestle into his chest. It felt right, holding her in his arms, her feminine softness against his hardness. He carried her to the bed, laying her down on the sheets. Gently, swiftly he undid his belt from around her waist. The turrets loosened, slipping them down her lovely creamy legs. Regrettably, he covered her again. He lingered a moment longer gazing on her lovely face before turning and striding out of their chamber.

~ * ~

"Jane, awaken." Oh, such a beautiful voice tugging her out of a deep sleep. Her eyes opened, obeying the command. She sat up dazed from sleep and rubbed her eyes. Drystan came into focus. He sat at the end of the bed. He was fully dressed complete with a sword attached to his belt. She frowned, realizing she was in his bed. Her legs felt oddly bare. She pulled the sheets up across her chest.

"You…you put me here." Had he taken advantage of her while she slept? She didn't feel like he had.

"What kind of Protector would leave his woman to sleep on the wash chamber floor all night?"

"Where are my pants?" She felt the heat rising into her cheeks.

"My turrets are where they should be."

Jane scrambled back against the intricately carved head board, dragging the sheet with her to cover what she could of herself.

Drystan relaxed back against the lower bed post, lifting his massive legs onto the bed, his polished boots hanging over the edge at the middle.

"Yesterday must have been…" he seemed to be searching for the right words, "…very difficult, frightening for you."

Was he apologizing? "You could say that." She drew her legs up to her chest, under the sheet.

"I have decided to give you time to adjust to my land, our ways, and become more accustomed to me."

"How generous," Jane said dryly. "Have you considered I don't want to get used to this place. I simply want to go home?"

"Aye, Blue Fire, you will tell me truthfully of what and who of great importance must you return to?"

Jane's mind went blank--this was her chance to convince him to let her go.

"I have…um, I have a business, people rely on me being there, and I have a job to do. I have…family too." The last part was half truth, as she had distanced herself from them with good reason.

"Any true family would not have let their daughter wander around alone, unprotected."

Jane just shook her head. "I told you my world is different. Women look after themselves. I look after myself."

"What stops the men from making claim to you? Are they all blind?"

"No, it's just…they don't…I'm not…" Jane stammered. Years of rejection washed over her, bringing emotions of worthlessness, loneliness to the surface. Jane's lower lip trembled. She bit down on it, fighting back the tears. "There's a certain mould men in my world want their women to fit into. And, well, I, I don't." She cast her gaze down, not wanting to look at him, wanting to hide the pain in her eyes. "It's complicated."

"Nay." In another instant he had shifted to her side. She felt his fingers under her chin lifting her face, forcing her to look into his midnight eyes. Warm tingles ran though her on contact. Would she ever get used to him touching her? She thought not.

"You gave me no reason why you should return. There is nothing for you there. The men of your Earth may be sublime fools, but I am not." Jane's heart pounded in her chest at his words. And his eyes, she would die a happy woman if she could gaze into their depths for the rest of time. Jane forced herself out of his grasp, trying to think clearly, a near impossibility whenever he was close to her like this.

"I know." She drew in a deep breath. "I'm different to your people. I understand you don't have a lot of women around. To you I'm just the current sideshow attraction. But I am nothing to get excited over. Trust me. For all you know I am the ugliest woman on Earth. That's why the men don't want me. And you shouldn't either." Jane desperately tried to patch the holes in the defenses he was close to crumbling.

"I see." He rose off the bed, standing to his full height. Oh gods, he was so dangerously sexy it almost hurt to look at him. But was he finally getting it? That she was not worth his attentions.

Jane rocked forward onto her knees, letting the sheet fall. Still in his shirt, its length covered her thighs and upper legs. She raised her right hand to him.

"This can be put on someone." She paused knowing her words would sting herself more than anyone else. "Someone better than me."

He stared at the bracelet. Anger seemed to darken his features even further.

"Nay, it stays." His intense gaze bore into her. "You stay."

"But, sur--"

"Enough words," he snapped, reached forward hauling her off the bed, and pushed her towards the bathroom door.

"Bathe, dress. We need to take you to Tuathal, make haste."

~ * ~

Alone in the *'wash chamber'*, Jane stood bewildered and saddened. She had tried to make him see sense, unsuccessfully. She blinked back an onslaught of tears. This was going to be harder than she thought. If she let him get too close, it would end in pain. Her pain. Shaking her head, she looked around the bathroom. Clothes had been laid out, soft feminine Kell clothes. Jane sighed. He wanted her to play the lady. With another frustrated shake of her head, she stripped off his shirt and hurried, using the *facilities* before taking a bath. She applied a lovely smelling substance she found in a small bottle on her hair, hoping it was shampoo. She might look like a horse, but she didn't have to smell like one.

Dressed, she twisted her hair up onto her head, securing it with a clip she had found among the pile of clothing.

Drystan sat at the table eating and drinking something sweet smelling and spicy. Jane's mouth watered. His eyes swept over her in appreciation. Almost anyone would look good in these clothes--they were low cut, revealing hints of flesh in just the right spots.

"Eat," was all he said as she sat down. He pushed a large bowl of warm, thick liquid before her. It looked like a cafe latte. She scooped it up with both hands, taking a sip.

"Ooh, that's good." She gave a moan of delight, taking a deeper drink of the creamy honey liquid. Jane tried to ignore his intense, heated stare as she sipped the liquid. "Why if you want me to stay, are you taking me to see this sorcerer?"

"We need to know if he can open a portal between our worlds."

Jane frowned in confusion. "I don't understand. What else could you…oh!" Pieces of the puzzle were starting to fit together. Here was a whole kingdom of strapping men and very few women. Earth had a plentiful supply of females. It made sense, but still…

"How do I fit into this?"

"You came though a portal. Through you we can open another."

So they did need her. And if they opened a portal, she could go home. All she needed to do then was get away from Mr. Large-and-possessive.

"What do you plan to do, kidnap a heap of women?"

"We would not take any mated ones," he said in all seriousness. Jane almost sprayed her drink all over the table at his words.

"I don't think you've thought this through properly. You know nothing about my world. You can't just waltz in and take women. The authorities wouldn't allow it. You'd have a fight on your hands."

"What would you do to save your people, Jane?"

It was an unfair question. Jane's shoulders slumped, knowing what her answer would be. "Well, whatever I could."

"So you will aid us?"

"No, there has to be another way. I don't want to be an accessory to kidnapping."

Drystan ignored her comment and pushed to his feet. "Come, we must leave now."

78

Jane thought about refusing to go, but she would probably end up being dragged out anyway. She sighed and rose to her feet to follow Drystan.

He stopped so suddenly, Jane almost ran into the back of him. He pivoted, swooping down, catching her around the waist, lifting her off her feet and into his arms, holding her tightly against his hard body.

Jane gasped in shock.

"I want you to understand." He bent his head, licking and kissing the side of her neck.

Jane was flooded with heat, her body turning to fire under his tongue. Of its own volition her head rolled back.

"From the moment I saw you in the woods, I have wanted you." He trailed kisses up her throat.

Jane shuddered.

"I feel the way your body responds to my touch." His free hand slid up the side of her chest, brushing her breast through the silk material.

Her nipples hardened. Oh god.

"I want you, not because you are an available woman. I see your beauty, your spirit, I crave to touch and taste you." His mouth came up close to her ear, taking the lobe into his mouth.

Jane's senses reeled, electric jolts shooting straight between her legs. She felt the moisture start to pool between her thighs, making her wet. She moaned.

"'Tis not a passing fancy. You are my desire. I care for no other but you."

Excitement, delight, dread all washed over her. She so wanted to believe him. His mouth found hers, plundering its depths over and over with needy desperation. Then, as quickly as he had started it, he dropped her. Jane almost cried out. Her whole body was alive, aching for more, her legs unsteady, her mind dazed. He held her hand, opened the door, pulling her along behind like a helpless little child.

Chapter Eight

It was a lighthouse. Jane gazed up in wonderment at the tall tower before her. She watched gentle waves roll into the inlet. Jane was puzzled--the sorcerer was a lighthouse keeper? Drystan shifted behind her as he moved to dismount, pressing his body momentarily into hers. It brought back the memory of his words with a sharp jolt. *"I care for no other but you."* He cared for her. But how? And in such a short span of time. Things like love at first sight belonged in movies and romantic books. Jane was a realist.

Over the past twenty four hours, her take on reality and life as she knew it had been seriously shaken up.

She was now formally introduced to Adalardo, the King. He laughed and made light of their first encounter in his chambers. Jane relaxed. He was a nice guy and King to boot. Instead of talking to Drystan, Jane chatted with Adalardo. He told her about his kingdom, how things were before the war with the Drac. She shuddered at the memory of the ones who had attacked them in the forest. Drystan's arm tightened around her in reassurance. She was safe with him.

"There are no Scoulls here. I will protect you," Drystan said when he felt her shudder.

"Hey, don't you mean I'll protect you." Jane was amazed she felt bold enough to teasing him. "You wouldn't have fared so well if I hadn't been there."

Adalardo gave a hearty laugh.

"Who taught you to fight, Jane?" the King asked.

"Well, on Earth women have to learn to take care of themselves. My sister and I had a few self-defense lessons when I was younger, just in case I got into a sticky situation. It was all very basic."

When Drystan moved to help her off the saddle, she placed her hands in his, sliding down the horned, half-moose, half-horse-like creatures they rode. She waited and watched as they had disarmed themselves, leaving their weapons behind.

"Your Sorcerer is opposed to your swords?"

"There is a spell on his tower. Any person trying to take a weapon across experiences great pain."

"Oh, smart man." She liked the sound of this Sorcerer.

"Do not be alarmed by Tuathal's appearance," Drystan warned her as he helped her across some large stepping stones.

Jane was expecting an old man with a long white beard, black robes, and pointy black hat. Tuathal turned out to be quite the opposite. Jane glanced him over in appreciation. He was handsome, with strong broad shoulders, and several long, deep scars, which enhanced his rugged appearance. One of his eyes was black and the other appeared to be an amber jewel. Jane was far from fearful as he stood regarding her at the bottom of the stairs. He held a long gnarled staff with a glowing amber crystal at the top. The man glanced between her two escorts.

"Tuathal, this is Jane Walker," the King introduced her.

"Wait out here. Jane, follow me."

Drystan clamped a possessive hand on her shoulder, stopping her from moving forward. "Nay, she will not go without me."

"She will be safe--I only wish to talk with her." Tuathal eyed Drystan. "If you want my help, you will comply."

Jane looked between the two men. But there was something odd going on here. She was feeling bouncy, light hearted, and very relaxed.

"Drystan," Adalardo intervened, "let him."

Jane just grinned at Drystan, skipping in after Tuathal. The door slammed shut behind her.

~ * ~

"Cool place you got here." Jane moved about the rounded room which looked a lot like a study. "Why do I feel like the world could come to an end and I wouldn't care?"

"'Tis a small truth spell upon my home."

"Like the no-weapon spell?"

He gave her a nod. "It seems to have affected you a little more than expected." His mismatched eyes regarded her with an expression she couldn't quite place.

"Honey, you've no idea. Right now I feel like I could fly." She grinned. Jane had never felt more relaxed around someone before.

Tuathal offered her a seat. She plopped down onto it. He drew a seat close to her.

"I have seen your kind before, human."

"Yes of the Australian variety. Go the Aussie!" Jane burst into a fit of giggles.

Tuathal expression was one of amusement . He gave a shake of his head. "And a very beautiful one too."

"No, no, no! Why for goodness sake does everyone think I'm pretty?"

"You do not think so?"

"Hell no. Are you all that desperate?"

"Jane, we Kells can easily see what is beyond the surface. You have a heart and a face of pure beauty." His words and the look of sincerity on his face touched Jane deeply. He reached out, taking Jane's right hand, bringing the bracelet into view.

"Drystan sees it too, or he would not have done this. If I had found you first, I would have done the same."

"Is that why everyone is hitting on me?"

The sorcerer's expression darkened. He released her hand. "Who has hit you?" he demanded.

Jane laughed at his somber expression. "It's a human expression not a physical act."

Drystan was pounding on the door demanding they let him in. Tuathal ignored the banging.

The initial giddiness from this so-called truth spell was subsiding. Jane felt compelled to tell him the truth no matter the question. It was oddly freeing as Jane took a good honest look at her life. Drystan did see her as beautiful and desirable. It was plain fact that Jane didn't have a life at all back on Earth. Drystan was offering her something she had always wanted. Why should she deny him? More importantly, why should she deny herself?

Because you hate yourself, came her brow-beaten subconscious. *You don't deserve Drystan.* I deserve to be happy. *He'll break your heart.* Everyone should take a chance even once in their short lives. The fact is Jane had always been too afraid to step out, try to meet a man, to try and be happy with herself.

Tuathal was staring at her again, a look she was becoming familiar with, a look of longing. These men were lonely, like her. These Kells needed companionship. They needed women. Jane had to help them.

"Alright, tell me about portals, how…" She paused to think. "How are *we* going to get women from my world to yours?"

Tuathal gave a nod with a half smile. "You found a natural portal. Many of them exist between many different worlds. The one you found connects our worlds."

Jane remembered the estate agent saying something about disappearances around Tindayle cottage. There was a portal there.

"Have others come through before? That's how you know about humans?"

He gave a nod. "You are the first one to survive the journey. It seems the fates were kinder to you than the others."

"Lucky me," Jane said dryly. She could have been killed, nearly was. Jane shuddered at the thought . If Drystan hadn't found her when he did, she would have died from internal injuries.

"Portals are made up of powerful energy rips that open the doorways. When you passed though, your body absorbed much of the portal's energy. So you are in a way a conductor."

"You have powers. Can't you open portals?"

"Aye, but without a conductor, or anchor to where you want to go, you could end up in any hell. This I know." He touched the scars on his face.

"Oh, I'm sorry."

Jane watched as he stood up, walked over to a shelf, and took down a small box. Returning, he opened it to show Jane its contents. Two beautiful jewels gleamed at her. One was a sphere-shaped sapphire. The other was a large tear drop ruby.

"I created these after the King and his Commander first came to me. This is a portal gem." He picked up the sapphire. "Hold it in your hand, envision in your head where on your world you wish to be, and the portal will open. But once you pass through it, it will close behind you. So you must always be the last to enter."

Jane nodded understanding.

"The energy you absorbed is limited. You are human and with my power I can give you two portals, one to your earth and one back to Kell. I must journey through the portal when you open it. Once I have the anchor to your world, I shall be able to create the portals between our two spheres."

"So, we need you to come. But isn't it dangerous considering the last one almost killed me?"

Tuathal shook his head. "Nay, you, and any others will be safe." He gave her a smile which enhanced his handsome face. "The other is an enchanted heart stone." He laid the sapphire down, handling the ruby. This one he placed into her palm of her hand.

It felt warm, and Jane watched with amazement as the ruby began to glow. "It will do that every time you find a woman who will be accepting of our land and our ways. I did not need a heart stone to know you already were, Jane."

She smiled at his compliment. "So why do I have to find these women?"

"It is your world. We assume you would know where to find unprotected women."

"It's usually traditional for men to find their own brides."

Tuathal's expression turned into one of confusion. "Once you have the means to travel to and from Earth then why not just escort Kell men over to find a single lady to bring back to Kell?"

"Your idea may hold merit, but I do not wish to be portal keeper. Kell men do not know the customs of your world."

Jane raised an eyebrow. "I can understand the customs bit, but you not wanting to play portal keeper, I don't. I thought you wanted to help your people."

"Jane, nothing comes without a price."

Jane studied the Sorcerer. It seems he had his own agenda after all. "You've got to be kidding me. What do you want?"

"My price is simple; I want a Protected of my own. I would have had you, but I am not so heartless as to take you from Drystan."

Jane was speechless for a moment before recovering her wits. "Okay, then go find yourself one."

"No, Jane, the price for me to play portal keeper is for you to choose me a woman to be my Protected."

His 'price' didn't sit well with Jane. "But what if I choose someone you don't like?"

The sorcerer shook his head. "You may not trust your instincts, but I do. Do this and all will benefit."

There was something this man wasn't telling her. Jane thought about it for a long moment. Before deciding it was a fair deal, she wanted to help the Kell people. How hard could it be to find this big handsome man a girl anyway?

Chapter Nine

A dark cloud of anger raged though Drystan as he paced back and forth outside Tuathal's tower. What spell had he put her under? Adalardo had walked back to the stags to wait. Drystan refused to budge. His woman was up there with an untrustworthy Sorcerer.

When her laughter had echoed down, he had tried to break down the door, but it refused to move. He wanted to know what Tuathal was doing to her. Was he seducing her away from him? He would kill the bastard.

Cursing under his breath, he went back to pacing. It seemed like a lifetime before the door opened. Jane stood there, her blue eyes gazing up at him. To him she was the picture of beauty, a smile lighting her face. She opened her arms to him to beckon him forth.

Although surprised at the change, he would never waste an opportunity to hold her. He swept her into his arms.

"Promise me one thing, Drystan," she said softly.

"Anything," he promised gazing into her blue depths, like a clear sky on a summer's day.

"Promise never to break my heart."

"Nay, Blue Fire, I could never do such a thing to you." Drystan pondered what had brought about such a change in her?

"Kiss me then."

A command he joyfully obeyed, covering her mouth with his own. He angled her head to push deep into her mouth with his tongue, tasting her sweetness completely. Finally, after a long moment he forced himself to pull his head back.

"If Tuathal even laid a finger on you, I swear I will..."

Jane's laugh cut him off. "You're jealous."

He frowned. "What if I am?"

"I like it."

Something was different. She had softened towards him. Indeed he was grateful for the change. He was simply confused by it.

"Tuathal helped me realize something."

"What be it, my sweet Blue Fire?" She was running her hands up over his chest. Her touch was bewitching.

"That you were right. There is nothing on Earth for me. I want to stay here with you."

Oh, the gods be praised. He could never let her go now he had found her.

"If you still want me?"

"By the twin moons and all that is holy, I want you, Blue Fire," he proclaimed before reclaiming her lips. He groaned when she kissed him back, her tongue shyly touching his.

"Huh humm." Adalado cleared his throat behind them. "Can that wait till we get back to the palace?"

Drystan slowly let Jane down but kept a possessive arm around her waist. She looked up at the King.

"Do you have news for us, Jane?"

She had such a lovely smile Drystan thought as she smiled at the King.

"Yes, I do. Tuathal has given me the means to bring you what you need. But I'm going to attach some conditions to them."

Tuathal came down from the tower holding a little box. He handed it to Jane.

"Thank you." Taking the box, she was grinning at the Sorcerer.

Drystan growled at him to keep his distance. She was *his* woman.

"Come back to me when you are ready to use it."

"Aye, aye captain." She gave the Sorcerer a salute and Tuathal chuckled.

Drystan tugged her away, keeping his arm around her waist as the three of them walked back to the stags. Drystan lifted her into the saddle, re-attaching his weapons before mounting up behind her. He liked the way she sat, her softness molding perfectly against his solid frame.

~ * ~

Jane was conscious of Drystan's hard erection pressing into her lower back as they rode to the palace. She found it hard to focus on the questions Adalardo was asking her. The feel, smell, and heat of Drystan made it hard to think of anything else but him. His strong arm like an iron band around her middle kept her pressed firmly against him as his other hand guided the horned stag. Oh cripes, she was wet, and almost positive she had soaked through her Kell clothes and onto the saddle.

Darn the Kells for not having panties. It didn't help that his wandering hand slid up and down her outer thigh.

"It is a good plan," Adalardo told her. "Each man and warrior alike can find his own woman to protect. I hope you will teach us Earth customs so the task will be easier."

"I, uh, um, sure," she managed to choke out. She couldn't see Drystan's face, sitting in front of him. She could feel his smug satisfaction getting her all worked up.

"Thank you, Jane. Your coming has single handedly saved our people."

Heat rose in Jane's face at the King's compliment. She was so unused to being complimented. "I don't think I had a choice in the matter, but I'm glad I can help."

Drystan's arms tightened around her.

"We shall need to call the Castes together. There is much to be done."

"Sire."

Jane trembled in his arms as she felt the rumble of Drystan's deep voice.

"The day has been taxing enough on my lady. A period of rest may be in order before we call upon her services once again."

Glancing at Adalardo, she felt the heat rise in her face once again as he gave them both a knowing look.

"Indeed, my friend. I would not wish to tire her out." The King's words held double meaning and Jane was acutely aware of it.

Adalardo was still chuckling to himself as they came into the stable yard.

Drystan lifted her off the stag. She looked up into his face, almost gasping at his hungry predatory gaze. Jane swallowed hard.

"Come, my Blue Fire." Tucking her arm around his muscled one he led her though the maze of corridors of the Crystal Palace.

With every step she felt the pounding of her heart, her desire mixed with a touch of fear. She struggled to find her voice. She had to tell him the truth.

He pulled her into their chambers. He closed the door, bolting it from the inside. Like a sleek, dangerous predator he moved. She backed up until she felt the cool stone wall pressing into her back. His arm descended to cage her in. His other hand gently lifted her chin. Their eyes locked.

"Drystan, I must tell you." Fear and desire made Jane tremble.

"Aye, my Blue Fire, do not be afraid. Tell me what is upon your tongue?"

"I...I told you no man has ever wanted me before. I...I mean no man has ever touched me either, no one but you." She watched as the realization of her words flickered across his face. The corners of his lips twitched up into a half smile. She felt his calloused finger tip stroked across her cheek and along her lower lip.

"This pleases me more than you know, my Blue Fire. No one will ever touch you but me." He stroked his hands down her throat. "I will be the only one to taste you." Drystan's head lowered, pressing an open mouth kiss to where his hand had been. When his tongue flicked over the pulse in the nape of her neck, Jane's knees almost buckled. "The only man to pleasure you. You are mine, Jane, mine."

Oh cripes, her whole body was hot, sensitive to his every touch. He trailed his kisses upwards. Jane tilted her head to the side to give him better access. The arm that had been against the wall slid around her waist, pulling her tightly against his hard muscled chest. His tongue found her ear lobe, sucking on it gently. Jane moaned when it swirled up and plunged into her ear. Jane almost came on the spot. Who could have thought Drystan's tongue in her ear could cause her whole body to suddenly ignite.

Her head reeled. She pressed herself against him with a desperate growing need. Jane was hardly aware he had scooped her up until she felt him laying her down on the bed. Jane reached out. She wanted, no, needed to touch him. Her hands found his bare arms and slid over his tanned skin before moving up to his shoulders. Oh god, she loved those muscles. Her sister would kill her in green envy if she knew the hunk she had scored!

Drystan pulled away from her. She whimpered her protest at his loss, watching him though half-hooded eyes as his sword hit the stone floor with a loud clatter. He quickly shed his clothes. He yanked his boots off, and then his leather pants. She sucked in a deep breath, as he hovered above her in all his sculptured glory, admiring his large bronzed chest. He had dark areolas and hardened nipples and a light dusting of fine hairs down towards his almost unbelievable eight pack. Jane was mesmerized by the way his muscles rippled with every move he made. Her eyes drifted lower before widening with fear and awe at his huge erection. Okay, so she'd seen pictures of naked men on the Internet, read many erotic stories, but it was nothing compared to the reality of his long, thick cock. It was richly veined with a rounded mushroom head, which seemed inflamed, almost angry. His slit was slightly dipped in the middle and glistened with pre-cum. Oh gods, it looked so big. Despite the aching need Jane felt between her legs, she feared it would split her in two.

As if he sensed her fear, Drystan crawled up her body tenderly, capturing her face in the palm of his hands. "Do you trust me, Jane?"

Looking deep into his black eyes, she could do nothing but trust him, the man who had saved her life. The man who desired her. The man she loved? The undeniable feeling swept over her. She loved him.

"Yes," she whispered, "I trust you."

His features softened and he lowered his head, taking her mouth in a deep intoxicating kiss. All fears swept away as his hand brushed up her arms, his tongue delving deeply into her mouth. Tugging at her dress, he peeled it from her shoulders, exposing her naked flesh to his touch. And touch he did--those calloused fingers caressing her shoulders running down her chest to take a breast in his large palm before rolling her hardened nipple between his thumb and forefinger. Jane arched off the bed and whimpered at the slight pain-pleasure sensation. His mouth continued to ravage hers, his teeth grazing her lower lip, biting, tugging at it. Jane moaned in need. He shifted her body under his, raising his own to strip off the remainder of her garments. Breaking from his lips, Jane gulped down air only to gasp as his mouth found the breast he had been tormenting with his hands. His hot, wet mouth sucked at her breast, tongue flicking over her nipple, over and over. Jane found it impossible to calm her breathing as his other hand snaked down her belly, down through into her soft curls. His finger found her hard, swollen clit. Jane jerked as he ran his fingers in tight circles. Moaning, whimpering, the pressure building built like a coiled spring. He pressed harder on her clit. When a finger found her dripping wet pussy, he plunged it inside her. He finger fucked her in a slow torturous rhythm as he sucked on her breast.

"Oh god, Drystan!" Crying out when he added a second finger, Jane's whole sex-starved body released, spasming hard around his fingers as she came.

"Yes, my love, so beautiful." She was barely aware he had moved down her body, stroking it tenderly. Jane was still shuddering from her climax. Drystan pushed her legs wide. His face disappeared between her legs. Jane almost screamed when she felt his tongue delve deep into her pussy, lapping up her juices. His hand held her hips firmly in place as he sucked, licked, and tongue fucked her. He growled against her. She felt the vibrations right through her core. Riding on the wave of her first climax, he was quickly pushing her towards a second. When his tongue slid up over her clit, Jane cantered off the bed, screaming as the intense explosion ripped though her body. Drystan did not let up on her ravaged body as he plunged three thick fingers inside her. Stretching her, he pushed them deep, filling her. Jane felt a slight burning as he pulled his fingers out before pushing them back in again and again, scissoring them slowly, getting her used to the thickness. He kept her there, peaking as he moved up over her. His fingers withdrew. Jane whimpered, feeling their loss. But something else pushed against her virginal entrance. Oh god, Jane had never wanted anything so desperately--to have him fill her. Arching her hips, she urged him forward.

"Open your eyes, Jane." The command penetrated her passion-drugged senses. She obeyed. Their eyes locked then he moved his arms up around her head holding her body tightly as she felt him push forward. Eyes widening, she felt him starting to fill her. Her inner walls giving way as his thick cock started to stretch her until he hit her barrier. Her whole body was shaking. still riding out the second climax. Drystan suddenly plunged himself in to the hilt. Jane screamed again, bucking, convulsing at the intense burning pain, with her third climax. Drystan remained still as the pain faded. Oh, never had she felt so full, or so stretched.

"Jane, my sweet beautiful Blue Fire Jane," he cooed in a strained voice as she slowly came down. A thin gleam of sweat coated her body. "So tight, so good," he groaned.

Oh god, it was driving Jane insane. She had to feel him move. Whimpering, she tried to shift her hips. Drystan groaned but seemed to get the message. Gasping at the slick, tight friction in her pussy, he pulled almost all the way out before plunging back in. He impaled her again and again in slow agonizing thrusts. Jane sensed he was holding back. As if he feared he would harm her. She reached out, grabbing his hair, tugged him down, and kissed him fiercely.

"Fuck me, Drystan, I won't break!" Her words seemed to melt his resolve. He gripped her under her knees, bending her body back as he slammed into her hard, gathering speed with each deep, penetrating stroke. The head of his large, thick cock hit just the right spot, time and time again. Jane fisted the sheets as the building pressure began to swell again, more intense than the last three times. Her hoarse voice cried out Drystan's name over and over as he fucked her to oblivion. Stars exploded behind Jane's eyes. Coming for the fourth time, her body was wracked with tremors. Her inner walls squeezed, convulsing around his hard, plunging cock. He kept thrusting hard, deep, so fast. He stiffened, roaring out his release, feeling his hot seed spurting forth deep within her womb. Drystan collapsed on top of her.

"By the gods, woman," he panted, lifting himself slightly so not to crush her.

She felt him slowly withdraw from her body, leaving her feeling empty.

"Never in all my days have I felt such fire."

Jane's whole body felt limp and boneless. Drystan rolled to his side and tugged her into his arms. Jane snuggled against him, the heavy sedation of sleep stealing over her.

"I love you, Drystan," she murmured into his chest as she fell into a deep, contented sleep.

Chapter Ten

"Oh, that feels good." Jane opened an eye to appreciate Drystan's glorious naked form as he slipped into the large rounded bathing pool. Her body was still aching and sore after the midday exertions. Drystan had gently woken her with a trail of kisses along her neck and down to her breasts, teasing her aroused flesh before scooping her up, carrying her into the wash chamber, and lowering her into the soothing, warm water.

"You feel good, my Blue Fire," Drystan said, reaching for her to tug her into his arms so her naked back nestled against his aroused front.

Jane giggled. "Your little commander should be registered as a lethal weapon." She wiggled her ass against his large cock. She was delighted when he groaned and growled in her ear.

"Take care, my love. I know you are tender, and I may not be able to control myself if you keep moving." His arm banded around her waist to keep her still. But he did not play fair--she felt his hot breath on the side of her face as his teeth grazed her ear lobe. Her lower stomach quivered. Moaning as his tongue swirled into her ear, she felt her toes curl with the deep passion surging through her. He had turned her into a quivering blob. His other hand squeezed and stroked her breasts.

"Magnificent." He breathed into her ear. Jane didn't care how sore she was, she wanted Drystan again. Now she knew what she had been missing out on all these years, Jane was determined to make up for lost time. Two could play at this game. Jane reached behind her to where his cock was pressed against her lower back, and encircled her fingers around his thickness. She gave a triumphant smile when she heard him moan as she gently squeezed. Her fingers were barely able to fit around him as she stroked him up and down.

He squeezed tighter on her breast, pinching at her nipples. Loosening his hold, Drystan pushed her forward to twist her around on his lap before pulling her against him again. Jane slid her arms up around his neck, her legs straddling him as he sat on the pool shelf, coming nose to nose. Jane grinned, reaching up to run her fingers through his thick black hair, loving the feel of the strands gliding though her fingers. She lowered her head to kiss along his strong jaw line. His arms tightened around her, his cock pushing against her mound. Jane wantonly shifted her hips to rub against him.

"Blue Fire." He growled, his midnight eyes heavy with desire. He gripped her hips. "By the goddess, I must have you again. Yet I have no desire to hurt you."

"I'm alright Drystan. I want you too. Any pain is fleeting with the pleasure you bring me." Jane gazed into his face, letting him see her sincerity.

He growled again, hand emerging from the water to grip the back of her head, jerking her forward to slam his mouth to hers in a

punishing kiss. Jane moaned into his mouth as his tongue ravaged her mouth. She felt him lift her, guiding her down over his hard, thick cock. Jane groaned at the intense sensation of being completely impaled. She winced at the slight discomfort of her tender inner walls being forced open. Oh god, he felt so darn good! Gripping her hips firmly, he pulled her up before slamming her down again, sending water sloshing up the sides of the pool. Drystan settled into a hard, fast rhythm. Jane lifted her hips in time with his thrusts, meeting him stroke for stroke as the pressure built inside her. His tongue plunged in time with his thrust. Jerking her head back, she gasped for air as he pushed her closer to the edge. He growled again. Jane arched her back as he caught a breast in his mouth, tugging on the nipple between his teeth. It was all Jane needed as stars exploded behind her eyes. Crying out, she clung to her lover as he thrust faster, her inner vaginal walls clenching down around his cock. Drystan's muscles tensed under her hands as he roared, shooting his seed deep inside her. She fell forward, her head resting on his shoulder. As they both struggled to bring their breathing under control, his hands gently traced the curve of her spine.

Jane raised her head as Drystan gave a soft chuckle.

"Aye, my Blue Fire, we had best bathe before the night's festivities."

Jane gave him a grin. "It's not my fault you're irresistible. Such tasty brawn and muscle, how's a girl meant to resist such delights?" He raised an amused dark eyebrow. Her face felt flush with passion.

"Was it just last eve you did not desire my delights?" The rascal was teasing her.

Jane slapped at his chest. "A girl's got a right to change her mind." Jane gasped as he slowly lifted her off him setting her down to his left.

"Aye, what did change your mind? I want to hear all what Tuathal did, Jane. Leave no part out this time."

~ * ~

Jane related the whole conversation. Drystan's mood darkened. He struggled to keep a tight rein on his rage over Tuathal's advances. And the price he had given to his woman.

"You can't blame him. I see the need you have here, and it is a small price to pay."

"He should not have burdened you with such a task." He continued to wash Jane's skin, enjoying the way that every inch of her body was accessible. He took pleasure in caring for her.

"I don't mind. It's probably a good thing. I get to go back to Earth."

Drystan stiffened at her words; did she still wish to leave him? "You are mine, Jane. I will not let you go."

Raising her blue eyes to meet his, she lifted her hand and ran her soft fingers along the side of his jaw. "I don't want to let you go either." She pressed her soft body against his.

He held her close against his chest. "I want to stay here, and I want to be yours forever. I don't know how it has happened so quickly, but I love you. Tuathal's truth spell was a blessing in disguise as it forced me to be honest with myself."

It seemed he owed a debt to the sorcerer after all. He tightened his hold, stroking her hair. The surge of unaccustomed emotion was strong.

He had loved her from the first moment he had held her in his arms, awakening his possessive and protective instincts.

"Aye, my Blue Fire, my heart is yours. You have captured me as much as I have you."

Her smile was radiant.

"'Tis my solemn vow to always protect and love you for the rest of time. We are bonded now, Jane. Nothing can part us." This he vowed with his entire being.

~ * ~

Once they were dried and dressed, Drystan pulled his jeweled dagger from his weapons chest. It had been a gift from his mother when he had first entered warrior training. Jane was twisting her hair back, securing it with a scarf. He watched her for a moment--the beautiful curve of her body, lust surging straight to his cock. By the moons of Kell, she was so temping. Drystan drew in a deep breath before coming up behind her, enjoying the way her breath quickened as he drew nearer. He bent to kiss the nape of her neck, feeling her body shiver. He knew it was not from any chill. No woman had ever been so responsive to him. She was indeed his perfect fit.

"It is my duty to protect you, but I wish you to have this in the hope you may never have to use it again." He placed the dagger into her small hands.

Her fingers curled around the hilt, Jane turned in his arms, lifting her gaze to show her expression of uncertainty. "Drystan, I don't know what to say. I mean last time I used this..." She gave a shudder. He pulled her into his arms. She laid her head on his chest.

"'Tis just an extra measure to ensure your safety, my love. Keep it close." He felt her nod against his chest. "Come now, we best not be late for the king's banquet."

~ * ~

"There you are, my dear!" Vanora gripped Jane into a bear hug, tugging her away from Drystan and Adalardo. Drystan gave an approving nod, and Jane let herself be led away to walk around the hall. "My, how lovely you look. Seems the way of the Kell suits you. I hope the Commander has not been too taxing on you my dear, being so small you must tire easily."

Jane felt her cheeks burn. "I'm good, tougher than I look, but thank you for your concern."

"Oh, look how beautiful," Vanora grabbed Jane's wrist to examine the bracelet. "I remember my first promise bracelet, and the joy I felt at belonging to my Warrior. It made my sisters envious. The Commander is a fine man, my dear, as I'm sure you now know. Before the tragedy of the Drac attack, many of the ladies had their eye on the Commander, hoping to be his Protected." Vanora chatted on as the room filled, mainly with men whose eyes swept over Jane with longing looks. When they spotted her bracelet, they moved on. Jane was more than thankful she wore Drystan's claim.

"Vanora, Drystan hasn't told me what is involved in being his Protected. Is it the same as being a wife or a girlfriend? Um how does it work here?"

Vanora seemed more than happy to explain the ceremony process. "Once the promise bracelet is accepted, the lady simply moves in with her man, under his protection. There they remain in a permanent bonding."

"So I'm already Commander Drystan's wife?"

"Yes, my dear, you are his Protected, if wife is what you call it on your world."

Her kind smile was comforting. Elation bubbled through her as she realized she and Drystan were married in the Kell sense of the word. She was married! Jane suppressed the urge to laugh with joy.

"What if, you know, they find they cannot stand each other after a while, are there any separations?"

Vanora looked perplexed at the suggestion. "No, my dear. Never a thing has occurred in Kell. Is this what the men may do to the women on your world?"

Jane smiled. "Not always the men, I'm sad to say."

"The Kell know their hearts my dear, so too the hearts of others. It is a beautiful thing."

"I am glad and happy to be here in Kell."

The large woman gave her another squeeze. "As am I. We shall have so much to discuss. You must help us prepare the palace and villages if more ladies from your world are to be coming to Kell. Everyone is talking about it."

"I'll do what I can," Jane promised.

Adalardo and Drystan came back to claim Jane's attention and to introduce her to the caste heads. Everyone was eager to learn about Earth. They kept Jane talking by peppering her with question after question until Drystan told them to stop. She was grateful for his intervention.

Jane sat to the King's left with Drystan on the right. Then the meal was served. Jane was hungry after skipping lunch. She ate everything that was set before her, stopping just before her stomach became too full, washing it all down with lots of sweet Kell wine.

Jane was thoroughly enjoying herself. She couldn't remember when she had had so much fun, enjoying the witty company of the King. Drystan was constantly staring at her as if he would leap over the table at any given moment and take her right there. She was wet just thinking about it. She struggled to keep her attention on the King. The conversation turned to the Drac and the war.

"How long have the Drac and Kell been at war?"

"For longer than anyone can remember now," Adalardo answered. "You see, the Drac have longer life spans than the Kell do and feel they are the superior species. Norlac, the leader of the Drac, desires power and dominance over all the land. His hate and greed know no bounds."

"War is a terrible thing in any land. My world is constantly ravaged by wars around the planet."

"There is war in your land?" the King asked.

"Not where I live but on other parts of the Earth. Greedy men, territory disputes--it seems some men will go to war for the weakest of reasons. It sometimes makes me ashamed to be a part of the human race when things like that happen."

"Be at ease, Jane." Adalardo smiled. "If other humans are like you, with much beauty and compassion, there is much to be admired."

Jane felt the heat rise in her cheeks at his words--she was so unused to compliments.

Adalardo continued, "Some things are beyond our control so we should never be ashamed of who we are, even if we dislike the things which others do."

"Thank you, your Highness." Jane smiled at the King. Glancing past the King at Drystan who held a dark jealous expression. Jane just winked at him.

"Nay, we should thank you, Jane. Without you, our people would be doomed to die out."

The King rose and the crowd hushed. Jane watched as he picked up his crystal wine goblet.

"Friends, it is good to be able to celebrate the hope which has come to us through the Lady Jane. Commander, you are the envy of every man in the kingdom as Protector of your fine lady. May you both prosper and bring many children to fill the palace's halls."

Jane blushed. Drystan gave a nod.

"It is just the first of many celebrations as soon each and every man will get the chance to choose a new mate. Our lands will prosper once again." Loud murmurs of agreement came from along the table. The King tilted his goblet towards her. "To the Lady Jane, bringer of hope and women to Protect."

Jane hated being the centre of attention but was slowly warning to it. As she smiled, her eyes met Drystan's, seeing the great pride for her in his dark gaze. It felt so good to have meaning and purpose. Without Drystan, she would have never known this feeling. She had placed her entire world in his strong hands. And never had anything felt so right.

Chapter Eleven

"You've had too much wine, my Blue Fire." Drystan steadied Jane as she giggled and swayed on her feet.

"I'm not used to drinking, but I feel wonderful." Her little hands were exploring his chest. "Hummmm, you feel wonderful." Drystan's cock had been rigid all night watching his woman's smiles, her blushes, listening to her musical voice. "I want to touch you," she murmured, trying to tug up his tunic top. Drystan gave a groan. He wrapped his arms around her waist to lift her up into his arms. Loving the way she felt there, he silently praised the gods for sending him his light, little Jane. He had to get out of the halls, out of view of any others who might pass by.

"Then we best return to our chambers with haste, lest I lose my control and take you right here, my love." Giggling again, she lifted her head, pressing her lips to his neck, trailing little kisses along his throat. Drystan groaned again when her hot, wet tongue flicked across his skin. His whole body was on fire for her. Damn, she was sweeter than the wine they had drunk, more intoxicating, more addictive than any taste he had ever known. He quickly walked the corridors, his cock straining to be free of his turrets. He almost came on the spot when the little vixen bit down on the juncture between his neck and shoulders.

"By the gods, Jane!" he gasped. Drystan ran the last few yards to the chamber door. It crashed against the wall as he forcefully kicked it open then slammed it shut the same way. She was laughing as he tossed her onto the bed, stretching her arms above her head like a languid cat. She gave him a seductive grin. One he had seen before, the first time he had kissed her in the Forest. Drystan made a mental note he would one day return there with her to ravage her on his furs. But for now his desperate need for his woman's luscious body was more pressing. Tugging off his boots and shirt, he cursed under his breath. It was taking too long. Jane sat up, slipping her turquoise dress down over her creamy shoulder. He stripped off his turrets. His cock felt like an iron bar as it swung free. Drystan leapt back onto the bed, entwining his finger into the fabric Jane wore.

"Too many clothes, Blue Fire," he growled. Jane gasped as yanked, ripping the material in two, revealing her creamy ripe, round breasts. Her nipples were drawn into hard little dusty pink nubs. "So beautiful," he breathed. Her giggling ceased and her eyes sobered with deep blue pools of desire. Her hands reached out to run over his chest. Drystan reveled in the feel of her hands on his skin. It was like liquid fire running through his body. He pushed off the tattered remains of her dress, dipping his head to her neck, tasting her skin. He sucked at the joint between her shoulder and neck before sinking his teeth in just hard enough to mark her flesh. She whimpered softly. Drystan knew he wouldn't last much longer. He also knew she would still be sore from him taking her maidenhead earlier in the day. Healing crystals would ease her tenderness, but Drystan did not have the control to go fetch them in this moment.

His need was too great. He pulled Jane further onto the bed, gripped her waist tightly, and rolled until she lay on top of him.

"I shall not take your tender channel, love. I shall take your sweet little mouth." Drystan watched her lick her lips with a wicked little smile. He pushed on her shoulders to encourage her down. Jane wasn't going to go quickly, no she started licking and nipping her way down his body, her fingers trailing through the dusting of hair scattered between his chest and navel.

"Sweet Jane, I will not last much longer if you keep that up."

She gave a lusty chuckle. "Hummm, but you taste so good."

Her lips vibrated against the skin of his lower abdomen. She was up on all fours over his lower body. She paused over his cock. He watched her examine it before gently running her fingers over it. He shuddered when her tongue slid out to swipe it over his swollen tip.

"By the twin moons, Jane," he hissed. "I am on a knife's edge here, my love."

She gave a lusty chuckle. "I've always wanted to do this, ever since I read about it."

Her lips were pressed to the side of his cock. Her words vibrated through his shaft. She mouthed and licked up one side of his thick shaft before repeating the action on the other side. Jane's small hand wrapped around the base of his cock. His hips instinctively pushed up when she sucked his head into her hot little mouth.

"Oh, fucking moons of Kell!" Drystan couldn't help the curse, cradling her head in his palms. Her mouth felt so good. Never had any of his past women pleased him to this level. Then again, none of the other women had been Jane, his little Blue Fire. Drystan wanted her to come before he did. He had to take control before she made him explode.

~ * ~

Jane gasped as he flipped her over onto her back, his huge body twisted as his legs and biceps caged her in. She stared up at his cock dangling like a delicacy in front of her face. Jane grinned, taking his cock head back into her mouth, suckling it. She let out a throaty moan around his shaft, taking it a little deeper as Drystan's face buried into her cunt. His tongue worked its way inside her, caressing her engorged, sensitive clit. Jane felt her muscles clenching at the sensation. Jane was finding it hard to concentrate as Drystan sucked and licked. Jane guided his cock back into her mouth and concentrated. Every time he sucked on her clit, she echoed by suckling harder on his cock. The action seemed to work to keep her focused on Drystan's pleasure. The fire between her legs seemed to spread through to all parts of her body. His tongue flicked over her clit before biting down lightly, shocking her into climax. Her orgasm gripped her, tensing every part of her body before she spiraled into the heavens. Jane's lips tightened around him, sucking feverously. He tensed a moment before a deep guttural moan tore from his throat. He spurted deep into her mouth, long thick ropes of cum she had to swallow quickly or choke. She struggled to get her breathing and trembling body back under control.

Drystan was the first to move, pulling her up alongside him, back onto the pillows. His lips swept gently across hers before kissing her on the lips. Then he pressed his mouth harder to hers, their tongues tangling, tasting each other's flavor. Both gave a moan. He trailed his lips down to her ears, holding her close against him.

"By the gods Jane, what you do to me."

"Well, I'm not complaining." Jane smiled, snuggling against his chest. He gently stroked her hair, sifting the strands through his fingers. "I think this is the first time in my life I've ever been truly happy."

Jane struggled against the pull of sleep--too much wine and mind-blowing, out-of-this-universe sex was catching up with her.

"I am pleased beyond words, my love." Drystan kissed the top of her head. "Rest now, my Blue Fire."

Jane had meant to question her new husband on why he kept calling her Blue Fire, but it could wait for tomorrow. Her eyes fluttered closed. She fell into a deep, contented sleep.

~ * ~

"Good morning, Lady Jane." Jane glanced up from her seat on the area wall where she watched Drystan put his men through their paces. Anyon leaned against the wall beside her.

"Hello, Anyon," she greeted. "Shouldn't you be out there?" She looked back at the sword play between some of the men.

"I surely hope not, little star. A twelve hour patrol on stag back is enough exercise for me in a day."

"Yes, I suppose so."

"May I say you are looking particularly beautiful in women's clothing?" He gave her his best charming smile.

Jane gave a laugh. "You may. But you'll be heading for another twelve hour patrol if your commander hears you," Jane warned with a smile.

Anyon shrugged before giving her a wink. "It would be mightily worth it. I have just heard of what you are doing for us, Jane. I wanted to thank you. And I hope when it is my turn to go to your world to choose a mate, she will be as beautiful and as fiery as you. I do not think Saraid's nose will sit straight ever again."

Jane laughed. "Then I think you'll be pleasantly surprised. Trust me, Anyon, when I tell you I'm a tame version of how fiery Earth women can be." Jane turned her attention back to her gorgeous warrior, watching Drystan and Adalardo spar, a thin film of sweat covering his hard muscled body. Lust for him surged though her body, making her damp between her thighs.

Jane had woken alone, but it hadn't been long before Vanora was knocking on the door to bring her three trunks of clothes, accessories, beautiful gold jewelry and breakfast. She had kept her occupied for a long time going though all the clothes. *Just more for Drystan to rip off*, she had thought with a smile. Vanora had also brought some healing crystals. She explained to Jane the power of the crystals. Jane flushed with embarrassment knowing only one part of her body needed healing. Vanora didn't say a word, instructing her to lie down so she could administer the curative. The energy from the crystals was surprisingly strong. She remembered feeling something like this not long before she woke up in the Blue Forest with Drystan. He must have used the crystals on her to cure her injuries.

"The Commander is a man very much besotted my dear." Vanora beamed at her. "Many of these were his family treasures. His mother was a fine woman, and his father was a strong warrior as well."

"Where are they now?" Jane asked before she could stop herself. Drystan was not a man of many words, but when he touched her, it spoke volumes.

"Sadly his father was killed in an incursion with the Drac. It broke his poor mother's heart to lose her Protector. She died not long after."

Jane felt for Drystan. "Sorry, I didn't know. He didn't tell me."

"Well, he has you now. By the looks of all this, he wants to spoil you." Vanora's bubbly, mothering nature was infectious, making Jane smile. Later she followed Vanora out to the training yard after assuring Jane she looked beautiful in a peach-colored tunic with golden combs in her hair.

"Lady Jane." Adalardo walked over with a handsome smile. Drystan was a step behind, glaring at Anyon.

"Your highness," Jane acknowledged with a smile.

"You are looking exceedingly fine today. Drystan, I almost regret giving her to you. You're a lucky man, my friend."

Jane raised an eyebrow at his comment. Jane could see Drystan's face darken with a scowl.

"My liege." Anyon gave a curt, respectful bow to the King before turning to stride away.

Drystan watched him go before turning to her. "What were you two talking about?" he demanded.

"Anyon gives his congratulations, Drystan," Jane said raising her chin.

Adalardo cleared his throat. "As much as I hate to come between new lovers, we have other matters to deal with." He looked between them--Jane's challenging smile, Drystan's possessive glare. You could cut the sexual tension with a knife. "Oh, the moons be dammed. Go clean yourself up, Drystan. Take your lady with you and be back out here in two hours. I want to establish a permanent portal between our worlds as soon as possible."

"Aye, thank you, my liege." Drystan spoke to the King but his eyes were on Jane. Her pulse quickened, recognizing his predatory look. Her stomach clenched, fresh moisture flooded between her legs. She never even noticed that the King had walked away.

"What did he mean, he 'gave' me to you? Hey!" Drystan grabbed her around her waist then she found herself flung her over his shoulder and marched back towards their chambers, ignoring the stares and smirks from the men who were watching.

"Hush, woman. We have two hours. I have no desire to waste time with talk."

Jane was happy to oblige.

Chapter Twelve

Once again Drystan held Jane nestled against him as they rode on the stag towards Tuathal's tower, listening to the musical quality in Jane's voice as she talked with Adalardo.

"Internet dating is all the rage at the moment--men and women use computers to find matches."

"These are strange words to me, Jane. There is much to learn before the men can travel to your world," Adalardo said.

She gave a light laugh. "I guess you just need to know enough to avoid getting into any trouble. Walking around with swords will definitely get you into trouble with the authorities, not to mention scare the women half to death."

They had just passed though a long field with tall grass. Up ahead was a dense, forested area. Drystan had been too caught up in listening to Jane to notice anything amiss until his stag pranced nervously. His eyes glanced along the line of trees. A sudden, eerie foreboding came over him--danger was near.

"Sire," he snapped.

Adalardo looked up and around. He sensed it, too, and drew his sword. Drystan followed. Then he spotted them, the unmistakable yellow eyes of the Drac. He counted at least twelve. There were too many to fight with Jane. He had to get her to safety.

He heard her soft gasp and felt her stiffen in his arms as a shiver of fear ran through her. He held her tightly for a moment to give her reassurance.

"Go, protect Jane, I will hold them off," Adalardo ordered him.

"Nay, I will not leave you." It was Drystan's duty to protect his King.

"Jane is our last hope. It matters not if I die today but she lives to bring us a…"

"No!" Jane protested, looking at Adalardo. "You can't."

Drystan thought quickly. He would have to send her to the Sorcerers tower. It was the only option. Tuathal's tower was close and Drystan knew he would protect her. Swiftly, he dismounted. He glanced up into her worried face.

"I don't want to lose you," she whispered. "You promised not to break my heart."

"It is a promise I will keep. Now go to Tuathal. He can send for help. We will hold them off as long as we can." He put the reins into her hand. "Can you ride?"

She nodded but was hesitating.

"Drystan I…"

"Jane, go now!" Drystan commanded, smacking the stag's rear and sending the beast bolting forward before she could utter another protest. There was one thing she could do, and that was get help. He watched her hold tight onto the reins. Leaning forward to keep her balance in the saddle, she raced across the field.

Jane saw two Drac jump from the tall grass. One threw something, hitting the stag in the chest. The creature gave a low howl and stumbled forward before it crashed into the dirt. Jane was flung from the saddle. Her right shoulder took the brunt of the impact. She rolled, momentarily stunned by the fall. Jane took in several deep breaths before slowly rising to her knees. The poor stag thrashed and whined. A dagger was embedded in the creature's right flank. Moving forward, she ran her hands over the stag's fur, trying to soothe the wounded creature. It grunted and panted, but stilled under her gentle touch. Jane sucked in a deep breath, curled her hand around the knife's hilt, and yanked it out. The beast howled, struggling to get up. Jane glanced up to see two Drac bearing down on her. Behind them she caught sight of Drystan, his sword swinging expertly as he fended off the small army of lizard men. Jane didn't want to leave. She wanted to fight--fight to save her man. But she was no warrior. The last battle had been a fluke--there was no way she could defend herself against the two Drac now approaching. Jane leapt to her feet and ran. Drystan was right. She had to get to Tuathal.

"Sshe'ss running!" one of the Drac panted in a hissy voice.

"Grabss her. Norlac wantsss her alive."

Jane's lungs burned with the exertion. Her legs were starting to tire. She suddenly wished she was a lot fitter. Hearing the footsteps pounding behind her, her panic rose. She was not fast enough. A scream sounded in her ears. Jane realized it was her own scream as a claw clamped down on her arm. She skidded to a halt, swung around, and thrust the dagger she still clutched straight into the Drac's stomach. The other Drac slammed into her side before she had time to react, knocking her into the dirt. His claw whipped out. Pain suddenly exploded across her face. She tasted something tangy and metallic, realizing with a whimper it was her own blood.

"You sshall paysss for killingssss him!" hissed the Drac leaping onto her. His second blow rendered her unconscious.

~ * ~

Adalardo stood at Drystan's back, his long blade held in a defensive stance, his eyes never leaving the approaching Drac, not even to watch Jane gallop away on his stag. She would be safe with Tuathal. They would dispatch these Drac in no time. The first Drac attacked. Drystan lunged forward. To stop the Drac's sword swiping down on his neck, he brought his blade up to deflect the blow.

WHOOSH! CLANG!

The air rang with the clash of metal on metal. Dodge. Duck. Deflect. Drystan swung his blade down. The Drac jumped back to avoid his sword-but not quickly enough. As it connected with the Drac's left shoulder, the sword sliced though its arm. It howled. Drystan bunched his leg, swiftly kicking the Scoull back, knocking it off balance before he thrust his blade forward into its stomach. He yanked out his blade to defend against two other Drac attacking him from the side. They were coming out thick and fast. Adalardo was keeping pace with him, cutting down and killing each Drac who attacked. The sudden scream of a stag made Drystan turn to see the beast Jane was riding pitch into the ground, throwing Jane from the saddle as two Drac were in pursuit of her. Drystan's blood boiled, his fighting became fierce. He had to get to Jane.

He lunged, punched, kicked, and sliced over and over, pulling a second dagger from his belt, plunging it into another Drac Scoull as it ran forward. Drystan roared in desperation as he watched Jane's now limp body being hauled away. He started to run full pelt towards Jane's attackers. The distraction cost him--he was hit from behind and pushed to the ground. Drystan twisted quickly to deflect a blow. Adalardo was beside him, panting as he lopped the Drac Scoull's head from its body in one clean blow. He offered his arm to Drystan, helping him to his feet.

"Go! I can handle the rest. Jane needs you," he ordered before racing back to attack more of the Drac Scoulls.

Drystan ran to where Jane had fallen, but she was gone, nowhere in sight. He saw that the stag was dead. There was also a dead Scoull further up the track. At least she had been able to kill one of her attackers in the process, but it had not been enough. Carefully, he scanned the ground, searching for signs as to which direction they had gone. Desperation, fear, and dread like nothing he had ever felt before coursed through him. He could not lose Jane when he'd just found her. If they had wanted her dead, they would have killed her outright as they had with so many of their women. This added a measure of hope to his fear and anger. He had to act quickly or risk losing Jane forever. Something he could not even begin to contemplate. Tuathal's tower was not far from here. Drystan looked over to Adalardo who had successfully killed the last of the Drac.

"Gather the army. I am going to Tuathal. I know he can find Jane."

Adalardo waved his sword in reply then went for his stag. Drystan turned, launching into a full run.

Upon reaching Tuathal's tower, Drystan was struck by a sudden agonizing pain gripping his body. He looked down at the sword strapped to his side. He unhooked it along with his second dagger, quickly throwing them to the ground. He was within the range of Tuathal's anti-weapons spell.

"Tuathal!" Drystan roared. Free from weapons, the pain instantly stopped. Tuathal appeared at the door before Drystan reached it. "The Drac have taken Jane. I need your help to find her. Please, I will pay any price you want."

Tuathal mismatched eyes held no emotion. Tuathal regarded him for a moment.

"And if my price is Jane? Would you give her to me?" Drystan stared at the Sorcerer. There was no way in hell he would give Jane to another man. Drystan fought against every possessive instinct in his body to stop from reaching out to strangle the Sorcerer with his bare hands. He drew in a long, slow breath. Jane mattered more to him than the air he breathed. He would do anything to secure her safety, even if it meant giving her to Tuathal. "I will, if you swear on your life, everything you hold sacred, you will protect her, keep her safe."

Tuathal regarded him again. "Wait."

Drystan watched and waited as the Sorcerer disappeared into his tower before returning with his staff. He closed the door, and walked to the stepping stones, stopping when he reached the center of the causeway. Drystan watched as he dipped the amber crystal into the water and started muttering words Drystan could not understand. A small clear orb rose up from the water and flashed with images. Drystan moved in closer to see more clearly into the orb. But Tuathal raised his hand to stop him. The sorcerer's eyes remained fixed on the orb. Drystan's fists

120

clenched and unclenched as he waited for what seemed an eternity. When Tuathal turned, the orb splashed back into the water.

"They have taken her to Norlac in the ruins of his fortress."

Drystan leapt across the stepping stones. Tuathal reached out and grabbed his arm, halting his progress.

"My price, Drystan."

He froze clenching his jaw waiting to hear the words.

"I would not have taken her from you Commander. I needed to know the extent of your feelings for her. Besides, Jane would not have me. She loves you. You will keep her safe and happy. If I hear you have hurt her in any way then it will be my wrath."

Drystan blinked in surprise, looking at the man with a new respect.

"Remember she has her own price to pay to me."

Drystan nodded. "I will help her fulfill it," he promised. Tuathal gave him a bow of respect and released his arm.

"Go quickly now. You do not have much time."

~ * ~

Jane woke with a jolt. Her arms were tied behind her back, and she was draped over the back of a stag. The side of her face throbbed. Pressed into the moving creature, Jane felt nauseous coupled with the fact her head hung down, making all the blood rush to her brain. She groaned and struggled, trying to dislodge herself from the creature's back.

"Be ssstill female," hissed a voice.

She breathed in deeply, trying to calm the nausea. "Let me go."

The Drac didn't answer. Jane struggled again as they kept on riding. "Let me up or I'll throw up all over your foot!"

121

This made the Drac lift her by the waist and sit her facing forward. Its scaly arm banded around her waist. Jane glanced about, but could see no sign of anyone else, not even another Drac. Jane twisted slightly to face her captor. His yellow eyes looked her over briefly then returned to the path they were taking through a heavily wooded area.

"Where are you taking me?"

The Drac glanced back at her. Its eyes seemed to ponder whether he should answer her question.

"To Norlac."

"Norlac is your leader, right?"

"He isss sssupreme Ruler over all of Draconarr."

Jane wasn't certain, but there seemed to be a hint of loathing behind those words.

"Why are you taking me to Norlac the supreme Ruler of Draconarr, then?"

The question seemed to confuse him. "He hasss ordered you be brought before him."

"Why?"

The Drac gave out a frustrated groan. She was questioning him like a three year old child would.

"I do not asssk why. I obey."

"You do everything he says?"

"Yessss."

'*Go fetch doggy*', she thought. Maybe she could use this to her advantage. "Why?"

The Drac was clearly becoming frustrated with her 'why' questions.

"To disssobey the Sssupreme Ruler of Draconarr meanssss death."

"Oh, so if your Supreme Ruler tells you to cut your own throat, you would do it?"

The Drac shifted in the saddle. "I am Drac. I obey Norlac."

"You don't have to obey all the time. Ever heard of free will? The right to choose one's own path?"

The Drac kept its gaze ahead of them, pushing the stag to move faster. "We are Drac. You will be sssilent, female."

"If you ask me, it sucks being a Drac right now. You know the Kell are going to hunt you down and take each and every one of your heads for kidnapping me. My husband is Commander of the Kell warriors, and he won't rest until your head is on a spike outside the palace walls."

The Drac stiffened at her threats. "Ssssilence!" he hissed with more venom.

Jane inwardly smiled. She was getting to him. "It doesn't have to be that way." Jane softened her voice. "All you have to do is let me go and ride away. No one has to know. Not even Norlac."

The Drac was silent again.

Jane pushed further. "Don't you want to live your life in peace, without the fear of wondering if you're next to be sent to your death for a meaningless cause?"

"Draconarr is not a meaninglesssss causssse female. We are ssssupreme over all."

"That's all extremely interesting, but it's a bit useless being supreme over anything when you're dead." Jane's last comment seemed to have been the last straw for the Drac. Jane heard something being torn, and the next thing she knew a long rag was shoved roughly around her

123

mouth, gagging her. So much for plan A. Jane realized she still had the blade Drystan had given to her strapped to her left thigh. Obviously the Drac didn't think to frisk her for weapons.

Jane struggled to suppress her fear, weighing her odds of survival now the Drac had her. Jane had no doubt Drystan would come for her. She just had to manage to stay alive long enough for him to find her.

Chapter Thirteen

Adalardo had taken longer than Drystan would have liked to bring back thirty of his finest warriors.

"It is Norlac. She's been taken to his fortress," Drystan informed the King as he mounted the stag they had brought him.

"We destroyed Norlac's house of evil." Adalardo's face looked grim.

"Not well enough." He turned his stag north.

"We will recover her alive, my friend." Adalardo tried to reassure him.

But Drystan would seek no comfort until Jane was safe in his arms. Drystan let the rage take over his system. Selfishly, as much as his people needed her, he needed her even more. He was going to tear every last Drac limb from limb, starting with Norlac. He kicked the stag into a full gallop, the men following close at heal. It was time to put an end to this madness once and for all.

~ * ~

Jane's gaze followed the sky-line up the side of a mountain. The ruins of what was obviously once a magnificent fortress now looked burnt out and crumbled down. Stone lizard sculptures lay scattered. A major battle had occurred here. To Jane the land felt different here, darker somehow, like a heavy veil was covering the ground and its inhabitants. Jane glanced up at her captor, whose yellow eyes held no emotion as he rode up across a stone bridge and under a broken archway, stopping at two huge twenty feet double doors. Two heavily armed Drac stood guard outside. Her captor dismounted and grabbed Jane's hips. She gave a squeal through her gag as he tossed her over his shoulder, walking through the door the two guards had opened. Jane was bumped on the Drac shoulder as he carried her down a long hallway into an open, cathedral-like chamber where more Drac sat about. Jane managed to lift her head slightly to see the Drac staring at her as she was carried past them then down a long hall.

She heard a second door open. Jane was carried into a smaller chamber. The Drac lifted her off his shoulder and Jane found herself flung onto the hard floor. Lifting her head, she glanced up at a large, overbearing Drac. Jane would have been impressed by his size if she hadn't been so terrified of what he was going to do to her.

"Forgivess me my Lord, we did not kill the King or the Commander yet, but we captured hisss female asss you dessssired."

It was difficult to sit up with her hands tied behind her back but she managed. As she stared at the large creature, Jane could only assume this was Norlac, leader of the Drac.

126

"You may redeem yourself yet Scoull. I have no doubt the Commander will want to reclaim his female. You can kill him then." He spoke clearly without any hint of the hissy lisp the other Drac had.

Her Drac abductor bowed low to the ground before turning and leaving her alone with Norlac. She almost wished he hadn't gone as Norlac's large yellow eyes turned on her with distaste.

"I hear rumors you are going to save the Kell, yet you are clearly not one of them." He bent down.

Jane tried to scoot back from his touch. He grabbed her arms, lifting her to her feet and pulled the gag from her mouth.

"So small and pathetic. Where do you come from?" Norlac's eyes raked over her from head to toe.

"Yeah, well, you're not exactly a bunch of roses either," she snapped back, trying to tug herself free from his grasp.

He looked amused by her words and action. "Kell females at least had more stature than this frail, female body." He raked a claw down across the curve of her throat over her neck and shoulders. Jane struggled to hide the shudder of disgust.

"First, I have a name. It's Jane. Second, by no means am I frail. And thirdly, get your grubby claws off me!"

Norlac's claws tightened around the base of her throat, almost to the point of pain.

"Jane, of what land? Are there more of your kind coming to my lands?" Norlac persisted with the questions. He spun her around and sliced open the binding at her wrists.

Jane was thankful for having free arms. She rubbed her wrists to help bring back some circulation.

Norlac gripped the base of her neck and leaned down to hiss into her ear.

"I shall give you two options. Answer my questions and I may let you live. If you choose to stay silent, I shall inflict slow agonizing pain until you beg me to kill you out of mercy, but only after you have told me everything I want to know." He let go of her neck.

Jane drew in a deep breath, turning to face the monster who had ordered the death of so many women and children. Jane knew there were things she could not tell this monster. Her life was already in jeopardy, simply being here. If he knew what she meant to the Kell, they would not hesitate to kill her outright. Jane had to bide her time until Drystan came.

"Okay, you want to play twenty questions. Does this mean I get to ask questions too?" Jane was trembling, tying hard to mask her fear. Maybe she could get him talking, stall for time.

Norlac took a menacing step. She stepped back in fear.

"I ask, you answer, female."

"It's not very fair, I mean…" Jane gasped as he gripped her by her hair, yanking it back. Jane gasped in surprise and panic.

"Do not think I do not know what you are doing? What is your land?" His grip tightened and Jane whimpered.

"Earth," Jane squeaked in pain. "I am from the Earth."

"How did you get from this Earth to here?"

Jane had to think quickly, measure whether this information could be damaging to the Kell people.

"Please, let me go. I'll tell you."

Norlac released her hair.

Jane quickly put distance between them. "I came through a portal between our worlds, quite by accident." It was the truth.

Norlac paused as if he was thinking about her words. "Why have not others come through before you?"

"They apparently have. I am the first to survive the portal."

"Is this portal open so anyone may travel to your world?"

Jane shook her head. "I'm not a portal expert. I was told there was no going back the way I came."

Norlac circled her like a shark, waiting to devour its prey. "How can one lone female save the Kell from extinction?"

"Basic human mathematics-one girl and one boy makes three, so on and so forth. You're crazy if you think you can wipe out an entire species just by killing all their women."

"I will take great pleasure in watching the Kell die out. No one and nothing can stop me." His tone was malicious. Norlac grabbed her wrist, lifting it to examine the bracelet.

"The Commander is your protector?"

Jane bit down on her lower lip. She didn't answer. She should have expected Norlac's response to her silence but was caught by surprise when the back of his clawed hand whipped out, connecting with the side of her face. Pain exploded across her cheekbone and jaw. Tears sprung to the back of Jane's eyes as she bit back a whimper. Stumbling, she tried hard to keep her balance, tasting the now familiar flavor of her blood. He lifted her chin, his evil yellow eyes looking into hers. She glared defiantly back at him. She let her rage and temper surface.

"Commander Drystan is going to have your head on a platter for even laying a finger on me."

Norlac's laugh was menacing. "Much more fight than a simpering Kell female. I can see the appeal-which will make breaking you more enjoyable."

Jane clenched her teeth together.

"I still do not see the importance you hold to the Kell apart from being female. I want to know more about this portal."

"I told you. I came through one by accident. There is no way back. I'm stuck here."

Norlac grabbed her by the throat, lifting her off her feet. Jane struggled, tearing at his hand, her eyes bulging, trying to breathe.

"Liar," he hissed, tossing her backwards.

Jane's body slammed against the wall. Her body screamed in pain. She wanted to crawl over to Norlac, tell him everything he wanted to know to stop the pain. But she could not, she would not. Even through all the pain, Jane was determined to stay strong for the man she loved. No secret would pass her lips, no matter how much she had to endure from this psychopath.

"Tell me about the portals."

Jane narrowed her eyes, clamping her lips into a tight line to show her defiance. Her heart yearned for her man. Even if she had to die she would protect him and the people of Kell. Jane shifted against the stone wall at her back. Drystan had given her hope, courage, and self confidence. She'd be damned if she'd let this pathetic creature get the better of her.

"Answer me!"

"Go to hell." Jane spat at him. He stuck her across the face again. The whole side of her face throbbed. She whimpered, sliding down to the ground and spat out the blood that had pooled in her mouth.

Norlac grabbed her by the hair, pulling her to her feet. He had an evil gleam in his eye as his gaze raked over her body.

"Perhaps the pain of a Drac mating will loosen your tongue." He stepped in closer, grabbing her by the back of her neck. "When my cock enters your body, tearing at your soft insides, you will be begging to tell me anything I want to know. No Kell woman has ever survived a Drac fucking. I doubt your kind would survive it either." His claw sliced open the bodice of her dirty top.

No way in hell was she going to endure such a thing. She'd fight to the last breath. Jane quickly glanced over his body, summing up his physique. He was too tall to knee in the groin. Instead, Jane kicked hard at his ankle, remembering the Drac seemed to have a soft spot there. This made him release her neck. As he yelped, leaning forward, Jane slammed her clenched fist into his nose with all the force she could muster. He fell backwards. Jane kicked him hard in the groin, leapt over him and raced to the door. Jane had barely managed to yank open the door when the whole force of Norlac's body crashed against hers, slamming it shut again, knocking the breath from her lungs. Jane tried to gulp for air as he grabbed her hair, pulling her back into the room uttering a string of angry hisses and clicks of the tongue.

Jane managed to scream as he flung her backwards onto the floor. She was stunned for a moment. He approached menacingly.

"You shall pay for that!" he hissed.

Breathing hard, Jane twisted around, reaching for the dagger strapped to her thigh. Yanking it from its sheath, she held it tightly in her trembling hand.

Norlac gave another evil laugh. "You cannot fight me, little female."

"Yeah, we'll see." Jane climbed to her feet. Norlac lunged. Jane tried slicing at him with the blade, but he was too quick, catching her wrist and yanking the blade from it. She kicked out but he had anticipated her move. Norlac punched her hard in her stomach. Painfully winded, Jane struggled to breathe, collapsing onto the floor. Norlac was on top of her, pinning her down, his claw gripped around her throat. The blade she had tried to defend herself with would now be the cause of her death. In her last moment she thought of Drystan, the man she loved and prayed the memory would keep her brave.

Chapter Fourteen

Melor and Briac charged the two guards standing outside. Drystan kicked down the hall door with Adalardo. Warriors flooded into the open hall fanning out to attack the startled Drac Scoulls. They drew their weapons, jumping to their feet to fight. Drystan didn't stop. He ran forward through the burnt out fortress, his heart pounding with fear of what he would find. He would cut out Norlac's still-beating heart if he had hurt her. A scream rent the air. For a split second Drystan's heart stopped beating in his chest, knowing it was Jane's scream.

He sprinted down the last section of the hall, leaping to attack the guard stationed outside the door. Nothing was going to keep him from his Blue Fire. The Drac repelled his blade, fighting back with his own. But the Scoull's skill was no match for Drystan or his anger. With a quick succession of heavy blows, the Scoull was pushed backwards and off balance, leaving his underbelly vulnerable, Drystan did not hesitate, thrusting his sword straight into the Drac's stomach before kicking him off. The Drac fell heavily against the wall then slid onto the floor.

Drystan used his weight to crash open the heavy wooden door, barreling into the room. He saw Jane struggling beneath Norlac. A clawed hand gripped at her throat, pinning her to the floor. A dagger flashed in his other hand, raised to strike. Drystan charged at him, knocking Norlac off Jane. Norlac went sprawling sideways, crashing into the wall. He praised the gods she was alive. But when Drystan saw the bruising and blood on Jane's face, her torn clothing, eyes filled with pain and relief, Drystan's rage knew no bounds as he stepped between Jane and Norlac. He reached down with one arm pulling Jane to her feet and into his arms. Tears were falling down her dirt-smudged cheeks.

"I knew you would come," she whispered through her battered lips. The love for him shone brightly in her beautiful, blue eyes.

Norlac had jumped back to his feet and charged, still gripping the dagger in his clawed hand. Drystan pushed Jane out of the way to deflect the blade with his sword. He pushed Norlac back. He heard Jane's whimper, but he could not afford to look at her now as he kept his eyes fixed on Norlac.

"There is no escape this time, Norlac. You will pay for your crimes."

Norlac gave a menacing laugh. "You are all doomed to die out, pathetic Kells--no women from any land are going to save you. I shall see to it."

Drystan was not one to waste time on useless banter. He had come for one reason, Jane, but now he would not waste the opportunity to wreak revenge on all this creature had inflicted upon his people.

"It is over, Norlac."

He watched as Norlac walked over to a table, retrieving a long, jagged-edged Drac sword. Drystan recognized the dagger Norlac held as the one he'd given Jane. Drystan could only assume Norlac had taken it from her. Norlac was preparing to battle him. Good. Drystan was hoping Norlac wouldn't go down without a fight.

"Yes, it is over for you and your people."

Norlac lunged forward. Drystan had to use both hands on the hilt of his sword as he deflected the force of Norlac's attack. This left his side open and exposed. The dagger slashed forward. He arched his back a little too late. He felt the dagger slice through his shirt and flesh. The pain was fleeting. He strained to shove the weight of Norlac backwards. Norlac's experience and skill with a blade was far superior to any of his Scoulls. Drystan ducked as Norlac's blade swung with a *Whoosh*, narrowly missing his scalp. Drystan charged forward and straight into Norlac's body, grabbing at his left wrist to slam it against the stone floor. As they both fell heavily, the dagger spiraled across the stone with a metallic clatter. Norlac used the blunt hilt to hit Drystan on the side of the head, sending him reeling backwards. Both he and Norlac had jumped to their feet. Drystan shook his head, pushing back the pain. Physically, the warriors were evenly matched as they continued the attack. Drystan delivered a hit, slicing Norlac's arm open. The Drac leader grunted in pain and looked at the wound as his face twisted with rage.

The hatred poured off Norlac in waves as he charged again, managing to kick Drystan off balance. Failing to steady himself, Drystan fell heavily onto his back, knocking the blade from his hand. He did not roll fast enough as Norlac's blade swiftly descended. Drystan grunted as it sliced through the side of his stomach. Blood poured from the deep wound. Norlac tugged the jagged blade out, ripping his side even more. Oh, by the gods he had failed--failed to protect the women of Kell, failed to protect the one woman who meant more to him than life itself.

135

Mayhap this was his reward for his failure, death. He prayed Adalardo and his men would succeed where he had not.

"Oh, god no!" He heard Jane's cry.

He struggled, twisting around, trying to reach for his sword. Norlac was there and kicked it further out of his reach.

"You never had a hope of besting the likes of me." Norlac hovered above him. "When you are dead, I shall delight in fucking your frail little female. Her screams will be like music in my ears before I slowly slit her from throat to navel."

Drystan roared in anguish. He had to save Jane. He would not give up. Norlac raised his blood-stained sword ready to strike.

Norlac's yellow eyes suddenly went wide. His sword hovered unmoving just above Drystan's chest. Norlac jerked, stumbling backward before swiveling around. Drystan could see Jane's dagger protruding from Norlac's scaled back. Jane stood there, anger on her features as she lifted Drystan's heavy blade as she charged forward, impaling Norlac through his chest.

"No one messes with my man. No one messes with me!" she hissed as Norlac collapsed with an expression of shock on his face. Jane did not wait to watch Norlac die. She ran to Drystan's side, dropping to her knees he groaned in pain feeling her hand pressing against his wound to stop the blood flow. He gazed at Jane in awe and wonder. His wild Blue Fire had saved his life once again. Now she stroked back his hair, worry and panic in her eyes.

"Oh god, Drystan, hang in there baby, you're going to be alright."

He cupped the back of her head as she leaned over, planting kisses all over his face. Needing to feel her close to him, Drystan vowed never to let her out of his reach ever again.

"You are the wildest of blue fires I have ever beheld. I owe you my life once again."

Jane's wet lashes blinked at him as if something finally dawned on her. "So that's why you call me that."

"Aye, my love." He struggled to get up. But she pushed him back down.

"You're going to bleed to death if you move. We need some of those healing crystal things. There is no way I'm going to let you die on me. You're stuck with me whether you like it or not." There was a hint of panic in her voice.

Drystan gave a strangled laugh. "Aye, love, I would have it no other way." He pulled her down to kiss her lips thoroughly, pulling back when she whimpered in pain at the tenderness in her split lip. He gently touched her where she had been hurt. She gave him a brave smile.

Adalardo and Anyon burst into the door, skidding to a halt as they surveyed the carnage in the room.

"You get me healing crystals right now!" Jane snapped at Anyon, who looked bewildered at being ordered about by a woman. He nodded before running out.

Adalardo walked over to Norlac. Bending over, he pulled Drystan's sword from the Drac King's body, then wiped it clean of blood. "It is over. Norlac is dead." Adalardo drew in a deep breath, letting it out slowly as if trying to absorb the fact of Norlac's dead body in front of him.

"Yes," Drystan told him. "Jane has accomplished what we had failed to do."

Adalardo turned his eyes on Jane in surprise. "She killed him?" Adalardo gave a laugh. "Mayhap I should appoint you my new Commander, Jane."

Jane shook her head, a small smile playing upon her lips. All the while she kept her hand pressed against Drystan's side, worry in her eyes. "We have a small saying back on Earth, your highness, 'Hell hath no fury like a woman scorned'."

"Then remind me, Lady Jane, to always remain your friend." Adalardo walked to Jane's side to see how badly he was injured. Drystan was feeling weak and light headed with the blood he had lost. Anyon came skidding back into the room with the healing crystals, handing them to the King who quickly laid out the crystals then pulled Jane back to allow the crystals to repair the damage Norlac's blade had inflicted. Drystan closed his eyes, feeling the power of the crystals working their magic, healing his wounds. Although he was healed, Drystan was still weak from blood loss. His full strength would be recovered in time.

Slowly, he climbed to his feet taking in Jane's state--pale bruised face, her trembling body, small hands stained with his blood. She was so brave and so beautiful. Drystan pushed back his fatigue and weakness to take care of his Lady. Scooping her up into his arms, he carried her out of the fortress to where the men waited, cleaning their swords of Drac blood. Each man looked on with an expression of respect and wonder on their faces. No doubt Adalardo had already told them what she had done. Drystan lifted her upon his stag.

"Take the men ahead," he said to Adalardo who gave an understanding nod.

"Take your time coming home my friend," he said quietly before turning to shout an order at the assembled warriors. Drystan watched them ride away before mounting up behind Jane, pushing the stag into a slow walk. Jane pressed her face against his chest, sobbing. Drystan gently stroked back her hair, kissing the top of her head.

"Oh god, Drystan, I was so scared. I thought I was going to die," she gulped between sobs.

"No, love, you are stronger, braver than anyone I have ever known. 'Tis I who must suffer as I should never have let you go. This was never your war to fight."

"I love you, Drystan. I don't want to live without you."

Her quiet confession touched him deeply. Choked with emotion, he spilled the words in deep from his heart. "I owe you my life. My heart and soul forever belong to you."

She tightened her arms around him. Her sobbing slowly calmed.

"I now have the rest of my life to repay my debt to you, my sweet Jane."

He rode with Jane until he was out of Drac territory. Stopping by a stream, he lifted Jane down.

"My beautiful Blue Fire, I need to heal you now." He lay her down. She watched him silently as he washed her hands and face before taking out the healing crystals.

Drystan still felt the guilt for allowing her to suffer at Norlac's hand. There was no hint of accusation or blame in her eyes, simply love and trust. This touched him deep within his soul, giving him hope for a future he never thought he could have. Jane fell asleep as soon as the crystals had finished healing her. Drystan kept her close to his heart as they traveled home. A place he would always keep his little Blue Fire Jane.

Chapter Fifteen

How hard was it to find a woman for a dark sexy six feet-four man with the body of a god? So he had a few scars. Jane thought it added an extra aura of mystery to his outward appearance.

Jane wasn't in the least bit surprised to discover no one had noticed her missing when they finally made the journey to Tasmania.

With Drystan standing behind her, an angry Mr. Richards had been more than polite about her being late in returning the key, even gushing falling over himself to please them. She told him she wanted to buy the old cottage for any price the agent wanted, ensuring no more unsuspecting people could stumble upon the portal between their worlds.

Two months she and Drystan had been living in Hobart searching for the right woman for Tuathal, but Jane felt everyone she came across was wrong.

Flinging the file of the latest woman who had come into the office across her desk, Jane let out a frustrated sigh. The ruby had glowed beautifully in her hand, but she wasn't the one, Jane didn't know what it was-it was more a gut feeling which made Jane know she wasn't right. On the bright side, she would make a Kell man extremely happy.

Jane bounced down into the office chair of 'Ruby Glow Matches', the only dating agency on Earth which matched human women up with aliens. Jane was positive the government would have a blue fit if they ever found out. It was a step up from her cleaning business, even if it wasn't a profitable one. Jane didn't care about wealth as she was the richest woman on Earth and Kell having Drystan. Finding women willing to go to Kell on the arm of a hunky Kell man was easy. Finding Tuathal a woman was hard!

"I know that look, love." Drystan strode into the office room. Jane's eyes bulged in her head--the drool factor of Drystan in jeans was high enough to break the gauge. Jane wanted to bow down and worship the makers of Levi Jeans. Damn, he looked good--those huge guns of arms defined by a tight black t-shirt. Jane gave a smile, along with a lick of her lips, knowing all his brawn, muscle tall dark and very exceptionally tasty, belonged to her.

Drystan rounded the desk, holding out his hand. Jane willingly slipped her hands into his . He tugged her to her feet, drawing her into his arms. "I know how to make it better," he said with a satisfied smirk.

Jane couldn't help but laugh just before his lips crashed over hers. His large, strong hands roamed down her back to her waist. Jane gave a soft moan, melting into him. If she could bottle Drystan's cure for bad moods, then Jane would make an absolute fortune. Mind you, she didn't want to share her man with anyone. Much to Jane's surprise and disappointment, he pulled away.

"Hey, you can't get me all worked up then leave me," she said, pouting at her Protector, her husband, and the father of their child now growing within her.

"Aye, love." He gave a wicked smile. "Do I ever leave anything unfinished?" he asked in all sincerity. Jane knew he was always a man of his word, touch, and oh so much more. She shook her head. There must be a reason for him stopping.

"There be a lady in the waiting room to see you."

Jane knew Drystan's appearance around the neighborhood helped to draw women in like bees to honey. She wasn't in the least bit phased by it--she was secure in the fact her lover was committed to the last, and continued to prove how much he loved and adored her every day.

"I don't have anyone scheduled to visit, could be just a drop in." With twelve successful matches, Jane was feeling a rather self-satisfied match-maker and wasn't about to turn another potential match away just because she wanted a tryst with Drystan on the office desk. A special place which had been used for many non-office related desk-top uses since they had moved in. Jane gave Drystan a sexy smile. "I'll be back for you. Don't go anywhere." She tugged him down for another kiss before stepping away. Jane heard the creak of her chair under Drystan's weight as she strode through the office door with a sway of her hips. A movement which she knew drove Drystan to distraction.

"Jane, is that you? Wow."

Jane blinked at the woman with darker brown hair, deeper red highlights, and mirroring eye color. "Tamara? Goodness." Jane rushed forward to embrace her sister in a tight hug. Overwhelmed with emotion, Jane couldn't hold back her tears. Her pregnancy was making her overly emotional--Jane hadn't seen her sister since she moved out of their shared flat in Melbourne five years ago to move to Tasmania.

"What are you doing here?"

"Hey, no need to cry, I know it's been a while."

"Sorry, the baby is throwing all my hormones out of whack at the moment."

Tamara's eyes widened. "You're pregnant?"

Jane beamed a smile at her sister, giving her tummy a rub.

"Not that gorgeous hunk I saw just now?"

Jane nodded with a big grin. "My husband, Drystan."

"Wow and double wow. Hang on, back up. When did you get married? And how come we never heard of this? Mum's gonna chuck a fit when she finds out."

"If Mum had cared at all, she would have been in touch at least once in the past five years." Jane's tone was bitter. She drew in a deep breath to calm herself down. There was no way she would let anything get to her now. She had a new, wonderful future ahead of her, and the past could stay in the past.

"This all happened kind of suddenly." Jane had no idea how to explain to her sister that Drystan was an alien, let alone she got married on another planet-and she ran an alien match-making service for the Kell people.

"Um, well, it's kind of complicated. Come and meet Drystan properly. So what about you, have you got yourself a guy?" Jane didn't miss her sister's troubled expression as she tugged her into the office.

"Nup, no one. To be honest Jane, I've given up on love." Jane felt for her older sister, knowing what it was like to be lonely. Drystan stood up as they reappeared.

"Honey, this is my sister, Tamara."

"I did not wish to comment on your similarities, I had noticed." Jane smiled.

"Tis a pleasure to meet you."

"How did you score a hunk like him?" Tamara said unabashed.

Drystan smirked. He was still getting used to the human words and expressions that let him know how gorgeous he was. Then he would smile with amusement, sometimes even blush at the more racy compliments.

"Kind of complicated. I had an accident and Drystan came to my rescue, saving my life."

"Aye, then she saved mine, but twice."

Jane was staring at her sister's awestruck expression. Something else came over her. Jane's eyes widened. No, it couldn't be.

Drystan immediately picked up on her change of mood.

"Love, what be it?" He rounded the table to take hold of her arm.

"It can't be?" Jane gasped staring at her sister. The feeling was strong like a heavy weight lifting from her shoulders. Every instinct was screaming at her this was the one woman she had been searching for-her sister.

"What?" Tamara asked. "Jane you're kind of freaking me out here."

Jane looked up into Drystan's dark eyes.

"It's her, she's the one."

His brows knitted together in a cute display of concern.

"I'm the one what?" Tamara had a total look of bewilderment on her face.

"Are you certain?" Drystan turned his attention to her sister.

"I can't explain it but I know." It seemed good enough for Drystan.

"I am the one what? Jane, answer me!"

Jane stepped away from Drystan, catching her sister by the hand. "Honey, will you shut the shop, please." He nodded then strode off. Jane entwined her arm into her sister's, walking her towards the door. "Tamara, come have dinner with us. There is so much to tell you. And I just might have the perfect man for you."

~ * ~

"You're completely nuts-both of you .You've been watching way too much science-fiction if you expect me to believe I am the perfect match, not just for a man, but an alien man who's some kind of magician."

"Sorcerer," Drystan corrected helpfully. He'd just finished his third helping of the lasagna Jane had made earlier.

"He's an alien too?" Tamara pointed at Drystan.

"Warrior of Kell," he corrected again.

"Whatever, E.T," Tamara snapped.

"Tamara, don't be like that. I know it's hard to believe, but everything we told you is true. You'll see for yourself. Tuathal is due to arrive soon." Jane checked her watch. "Five minutes to be exact." Drystan got up and started clearing away the dishes.

"Oh, no, I'm not sticking around to meet another nut off your tree, Sis. Look, I'm happy for you and all but you're just plain crazy. Maybe you should write a book or something." Tamara made to stand.

Jane was quick to push to her feet. "Please, allow us the benefit of the doubt at least. If Tuathal doesn't show, then I promise never to speak of it again." She and Drystan shared a knowing look--never once had Tuathal been late on a portal run.

True to her word, a few moments later the large, swirling blue portal opened right in their living room. Tamara gasped in surprise, stumbling back a few paces against the wall.

"It's okay, Tamara. Don't be afraid," she said with a smile.

Tuathal sauntered through, making quite an entrance in all his Kell finery, his staff by his side. Jane thought he looked quite majestic and otherworldly as he stood in front of Tamara. His mismatched eyes swept over her sister from head to toe with a look of approval.

"I can run my clock by that man, I swear." Jane glanced up at Drystan.

"Lady Jane, Commander," he greeted.

"Tuathal, allow me to introduce you to Tamara, my sister."

Tamara was gaping at the large man before her. Tuathal smiled down at her.

"You have done well, Jane. I had complete trust you would find the one."

Drystan had come up beside Jane to slide a protective arm around her waist. Tuathal stepped forward, taking Tamara's hand in his, raising the back of it to his lips.

"Lady Tamara, 'tis a great pleasure. I have waited a long time to meet you. I see you are just as beautiful as your sister."

Jane chuckled at Tamara's dumbfounded expression.

"Um, thank you, I think."

Tuathal looked at her with a satisfied smile. He pulled out a small box from his robes and placed it on the table. "This will allow you to use the portal without my help. It will give you about a dozen trips. Use them well, until my return." He then turned his attention back to Tamara.

"Lady Tamara, will you come with me now?"

Jane was concerned for her sister's welfare with the sorcerer. "No protector claiming without asking first." She stepped forward, laying a hand on her sister's arm.

"I would never do such a thing. All I ask is you allow me the opportunity to become better acquainted. Let me show you my homeland, Tamara. I promise you nothing but safety and the utmost care."

Tamara hesitated. "Are you sure he's safe?" she asked Jane.

Jane gave her a reassuring smile. "Yes, go have some fun, I think you will like Kell." Jane watched as Tamara cautiously placed her hand in Tuathal's. Jane had a good feeling about these two. With an elaborate sweep of his staff, Tuathal opened a glowing red portal, different to the Kell-Earth portals. He gripped Tamara's hand tightly, drawing her towards it. The two vanished into the red mist and the portal closed, leaving Jane and Drystan alone once again.

"Something tells me the adventure is just beginning for those two."

"No doubt, my Blue Fire," Drystan murmured against her ear as he turned her in his arm.

Jane smiled lovingly into her husband's handsome face.

"Now, was there something else we have yet to finish." His lips worked their way down her throat, Jane sighed in complete contentment.

"Oh, god, I hope we never finish doing this."

Drystan chuckled, sweeping her up in his arms to carry her into the bedroom. "Aye, my Blue Fire, my love, we never will."

ABOUT THE AUTHOR

I live in a small corner of Australia, looking after three very active young kids and hubby. A dreamer who walks around with her head in the clouds, my kids and hubby often have to suffer a neglected household and endless talking about characters and plots.

Been reading books since I learnt to read, and writing ever since I could hold a pen. In my teenage years I discovered Romance Novels, then Paranormal Romance novels! I wrote my first complete work before I was twenty although it may never see the light of day.

As it does life often gets in the way of creative pursuits, but now I can't seem to put the pen or rather the keyboard down. I hope my imagination will delight and entertain others.

Other books by Angela Castle available at
Rogue Phoenix Press

Stealing Fire

Sequel to Blue Fire: In the land of the Kell, Tuthal and Tamara are content in their new relationship, until Tuthal uses Tamara as bait to steal back the soul he sold long ago.

Adalardo, King of Kell, has found his queen in Penny, an abused housewife from Earth. Adalardo must challenge Penny's husband in order to claim her as his queen.

The soul demon, who is angered over the betrayal of Tuthal, seeks revenge, targeting not only Tuthal but all those around him.

When the demon strikes a blow right into the heart of both men, they must join forces in hope of defeating the evil that has taken their women.

Regina, Reviewer for Coffee Time Romance & More gives *Stealing Fire* a rating of 5 cups and says:

"Stealing Fire has everything you could ever want in a fantasy romance! I absolutely LOVED it!"

Keeping Katie

Finding love in the boyish home renovator and handyman Jordan MaKensy, dominant lawyer Jack Cullen, will do anything to make their dream of a home and family a reality. When shy Katie starts working at his law office Jack, know he's found something very special, for them both.

Aussie girl Katie has come to London to start a new life for herself after a hard and tragic past. What she didn't expect was to find not one man but two. Katie is swept into a world of sensual pleasure that only two men can provide.

Yet Katie is resisting their attempts to win her heart. Jack and Jordan need to help Katie overcome her fear of love, to let them love and Keep their Katie.

www.ingramcontent.com/pod-product-compliance
Lightning Source LLC
Chambersburg PA
CBHW070332130626
46556CB00007B/2824